The Radney Riding Club

A book for all pony-lovers, with lots of detail
on riding techniques, jumping, gymkhana
events, etc.

Henry Thornton decides that because the standard
of riding in his district is so poor, he will start
a riding club. This news is enthusiastically
received, and the first meeting is arranged.
Although the members are all different ages, they
manage to get on fairly well, and besides
arranging for lecturers to come and talk to them,
they organize a gymkhana, and also take part
in a horse trial.

Josephine Pullein-Thompson

The Radney
Riding Club

KNIGHT BOOKS

the paperback division of Brockhampton Press

SBN 340 03812 8

This revised edition first published 1970 by Knight Books,
the paperback division of Brockhampton Press Ltd, Leicester

Printed and bound in Great Britain by
Cox & Wyman Ltd,
London, Reading and Fakenham

First published by Collins 1951
Text copyright © 1970 Josephine Pullein-Thompson

Chapter 1

HENRY THORNTON rode his bay thoroughbred, Evening Echo, up the mossy drive to the stables, empty now that his parents' and sister's horses had been turned out to grass. He led Echo into his box and began to unsaddle him, but Finch, Mr Thornton's groom, came across the yard.

' 'Ere, you'd better let me do that,' he said, 'or you'll be late for lunch again.'

'Well, they can't grumble, it's the last day of the holidays,' answered Henry; 'but, still, perhaps I had better rush. Thanks awfully.'

Mr and Mrs Thornton and Henry's elder sister, Elizabeth, were already eating shepherd's pie when he entered the dining-room.

'Sorry,' he said, flopping into his chair and beginning to eat at once. 'Echo decided that he wouldn't turn on his forehand; I had to stay there until he gave in.'

'I know it's not the faintest use trying to tell *you* anything,' said Elizabeth; 'but, all the same, I think you're absolutely bats. Daddy bought Echo as a good hunter and, considering his age, he is a good one, surely that's enough? Why worry with all this other nonsense?'

'Any fool can ride to hounds so long as he's courageous,' answered Henry. 'I want to be a horseman.'

'If it was polo, I could understand you,' said Elizabeth, pursuing her own train of thought. 'Anyway, Finch says that you're making Echo sour with all your messing about.'

'I wish Uncle George lived nearer,' said Henry. 'I need some good advice. Not your brand, Elizabeth; you're a defeatist; you don't try to improve yourself or your horse.'

'Your Uncle George is going abroad this summer; otherwise, you could have taken Echo over to Folly Court,' said Mrs Thornton. 'But there are plenty of knowledgeable horsemen around here.'

'It's cheek to bother people just for oneself,' answered Henry;

'but I think next holidays I'll start a riding club. After all, there isn't a pony club – and experts don't mind coming to instruct a lot of people.'

'Next holidays you'll probably have some other mad craze,' said Elizabeth.

'By the way,' said Henry, ignoring his sister, 'may I have Noel Kettering to stay next holidays? You remember, I told you about her – she's one of Uncle George's band. Her father's an archaeologist. He and Mrs Kettering are going excavating all the summer and Noel's got to stay with an aunt in London.'

'Yes, I remember; Professor Kettering's daughter,' said Mrs Thornton. 'Well, I think we could manage it, but only on condition you entertain her, Henry. You're not to disappear and leave her to Elizabeth and me as you did with that nice boy you brought back from school.'

'Oh, him,' said Henry. 'Well, he seemed all right at first, but he could only talk about school and three days in his company was enough to give anyone a nervous breakdown. No, Noel's not like that.'

Instead of packing for school, David Rice-Greene was taking a last look through his books on butterflies in an attempt to identify his capture of the day before. None of the descriptions quite fitted; perhaps he had netted something rare at last.

'Really, David,' said his tall, fair-haired mother in an exasperated voice, as she entered with a tennis racket and a school-clothes list in her hand. 'I've told you to get on with your packing a dozen times. You're never going to be ready for the two-ten train. All you ever think of is those stupid butterflies; such a silly hobby for a boy of your age. If only you were interested in games or riding; but butterflies – you'd better keep quiet about it at your new school or everyone will make fun of you. Now come on, have you got your games shoes? Two pairs of lace-up outdoor shoes, bedroom slippers; now your mackintosh. It's a pity you can't learn riding at school. I just don't know what to enter you for at the Waylebury show. Do you want to try the jumping again or do you think you'd better just stick to the races? David, why don't you answer? Oh, you are exasperating – you're thinking about butterflies again.'

Christo Carstairs gave her black mare, Dragonfly, a last pat and a farewell lump of sugar. Then she climbed the five-barred gate slowly. Looking back for a moment, she tried to impress on her mind a picture that would last through the long term ahead – a picture of a coal-black mare of 15.1, with an intelligent head, gazing after her with large brown eyes. Then she ran round the corner of the road and left the country behind her, for the Hill House, where the Carstairs lived, was at the end of Radney Avenue, a road on the outskirts of Trawley. Mrs Carstairs was waiting in the car outside the tall, red, ivy-clad house. Bill and Gerry – Christo's younger brothers – were swinging on the gate.

'Everything's in,' they called, 'except you; Mummy nearly went without you.'

'Good-bye. Don't overwork,' said Christo, leaping into the car.

'No fear,' answered Gerry. Bill was holding Sambo – the spaniel – on top of the gate and making him wave a paw.

'You won't forget to send me the schedule of the Waylebury show, will you, Mummy?' asked Christo, as they drove away.

'Oh, Oscar, please. Do try to be nice when it's my last day,' said Alex Turner to his fourteen-hand bay gelding. But Oscar made another threatening face and turned his hindquarters to Alex. 'I don't want to ride; I've only come to say good-bye,' Alex told him. 'Look, I've brought you some carrots.' He produced a paper bag. Oscar turned, and, for a moment, pricked his ears. Then he resumed his threatening expression. 'Give them to me or I'll kick you,' he seemed to say as he grabbed the bag. Aunt Esmé was calling from the garden; that meant that it was time to go for the train. He tried once more. 'Good-bye, Oscar. Take care of yourself,' he said, but Oscar turned his quarters again. 'I must go,' said Alex, and ran. 'You won't forget to look at his water each day, will you?' he reminded his aunt, as they drove away in the taxi.

Juliet Naughton didn't mind going back to school; she often found life dull at home with no companions of her own age – Roly, her brother, was only nine. She had no qualms about leaving Romeo, her light-bay gelding with four white socks and a blaze; he had Roly's roan Tomahawk turned out with him, so he wouldn't be lonely, and Daddy would look after them both. Daddy had also promised to clean her tack – she hadn't had time – and to take her stirrup-leathers to be repaired. Also to enter her for the Waylebury show. He was a very obliging father; in fact, she was very lucky in lots of ways, she thought. She always had everything she needed, from ponies to correct school uniform. Daddy had the car at the gate. He had left his business to take care of itself for the afternoon, so that he could drive her back to school. Mummy was ready; she was carrying a basket of apples for the people in Juliet's form to eat next day. Juliet put her tennis racket in the car and called to Roly; he was coming too.

Paulina Swindon had packed her trunk with her usual efficiency. She had reminded her mother and Mr Garland – the gardener – to bring Starshine into the stable during the heat of the day, to have her shod a week before the holidays began and to see that she had plenty of fresh drinking water. Paulina knew that they were not at all likely to forget, but she thought that if one was lucky enough to possess a pony like Starshine, a good-looking red-chestnut mare with a diamond-shaped star on her forehead, it was one's duty to make sure that she was being looked after properly. Everything was ready when the taxi arrived. Paulina took a last look round the tidy garden, bright with spring flowers, and gave Starshine a last pat.

'Good-bye, Mummy,' she said. 'Take care of yourself and don't worry about me.'

'Good-bye, old chap,' called Mrs Lawson, a weather-beaten figure in a tweed skirt and riding-jacket. 'Have a good term. Best of luck with the games; mind you get your colours.'

'Good-bye,' answered Eric Lawson from the corridor window. 'Thanks a lot; I'll do my best. Don't forget Choc-Bloc's oats.'

'Never worry your head,' shouted Mrs Lawson as the train began to move. 'I'll have them both as hard as nails.' She waved. Then, as the train was lost to view, she turned and strode out of the station to where the Ford brake was parked. He ought to win the pony class on Princess, she thought, and with any luck, the jumping on Choc-Bloc. She wanted Eric to have a really good season with the ponies, for it would be his last summer in juvenile classes; in the autumn they would sell both ponies for a packet and buy something bigger.

Helen and Jannice Barbersley did not spend the last day of the holidays riding their ponies – Swift and Swansdown. Though they were only day girls at St Hilda's in Waylebury, they had found it necessary to spend the day in preparing for school. They had devoted the morning to packing their shoe-bags and satchels; the afternoon to washing their hair, and in the evening they laid their school uniforms ready on their bedside chairs. As Helen, sitting at the dressing-table and deftly twisting her smooth chestnut hair into short pigtails, remarked to Jannice, they would now be in good time for the bus and would neither have to rush nor arrive at school looking all anyhow. As Jannice murmured in agreement, she wished that she had hair like Helen's instead of two mouse-coloured plaits that refused to stay tidy, and she hoped that the people in her form would be nicer to her than they had been last term.

The Marlowe children of Vicarage Farm were also at day schools. Fanny and Deborah were at St Hilda's, Deb at the junior school, and Graham, who was in between his sisters in age, was at Grantley Park. Mrs Marlowe did say something at breakfast about finding their possessions for school, but they all shrieked at once that they were going for a last ride, and she was much too busy keeping the farm accounts and breeding Dachshunds to bother about satchels and shoes. While Graham and Deb saddled Golly – a fat, round, black pony with a bristly mane and a bushy tail which they shared between them, Fanny raided the larder for bread and cheese, biscuits and cake. When they told their mother that they were taking a picnic lunch, she only said, 'Have a good time and don't be too late for tea.'

Chapter 2

THE Waylebury and District Show was always held in Stanton Park. There was usually a huge audience, but never very many competitors, for there were a number of other shows near by on the same day. In past summers Waylebury had always been one of Henry's favourite shows and he had never ridden home from it without several rosettes on Trappist's bridle; but this year he was too old for the children's classes and he had decided that it was no use entering Echo, who had never been to a show in his life and had been turned out since the Easter holidays; he would only misbehave. Henry was riding Trappist, for whom he was much too tall, in the Handy Hunter and Musical Poles, but somehow he felt bored with the whole affair. He leaned discontentedly against the collecting ring rope and watched Eric Lawson win the pony class on Princess; Stella Ridgeway, the daughter of a horse-dealer, who came from the other side of Waylebury, was second; Paulina Swindon's Starshine third and Juliet Naughton's Romeo reserve. Deb Marlowe fell off Golly; Tanzy galloped David Rice-Greene out of the ring and almost everyone cantered on the wrong leg. The Juvenile Jumping was the second event. Eric and Frank Ridgeway were the only competitors to jump clear rounds. Paulina – shouting 'Hup' at every fence – completed the course with two refusals and the gate down. Juliet forgot to jump the wall and was disqualified. Jannice Barbersley scratched at the last moment. David, Alex Turner and Fanny Marlowe all refused three times at the first jump. Stella Ridgeway's pony exceeded the time limit while rearing at the collecting ring entrance. Then Eric jumped again – this time on Princess – and had four faults.

It was fearful, thought Henry; only four people had finished the course and what his Uncle George would have said of their riding he shuddered to think. He felt the packet of postcards in his pocket; he had typewritten them with great care the day before. *Radney Riding Club*, they read. *Are you interested in forming a riding club to encourage better horsemanship in this district? If so, perhaps you would care to come to Radney Manor on 5 August at 2.30 to discuss the matter. Please bring your horse.*

He didn't suppose anyone would be interested, but he was going to hand round the cards. It was time somebody did something, he thought, as he watched Frank Ridgeway hauling his pony round and Eric, considered the best child-rider in the district, jumping with his hands glued to the pommel of his saddle. Eric was first on Choc-Bloc, the piebald cob, and third on Princess; Frank Ridgeway was second and Paulina reserve.

'Hallo, where's your new horse?' asked a voice behind Henry, and he turned to see Christo Carstairs on Dragonfly.

'Oh, hallo,' he said. 'Echo's at home. I've only ridden him twice these holidays, and he was pretty idiotic, so I thought that I had better not bring him.'

'Pity,' said Christo. 'You'd have won this class, I should think. Still, I shall have a look-in now; that is if this mad animal manages to behave.'

'Look,' said Henry, 'do you think that it would be a good idea to have a riding club? I mean when you consider the standard of riding and everything. After all, we've no Pony Club, and I think we ought to start something. Anyway, here's a card – I'm sorry it's so badly typed.' Henry thrust the card into Christo's hand and fled. He had prepared several little speeches in bed the night before. Each had stated the aims of the club in clear and concise language, but with a slightly different angle to suit the different people he intended to approach, but, when the moment had come, he had merely gabbled nonsense. Feeling depressed, he handed cards to Fanny Marlowe and Jannice Barbersley without a word and wandered away to saddle Trappist for the Handy Hunter competition.

A very ordinary horse called Susan, belonging to a fat man called Mr Galloway, won the hunter class. Mr Ridgeway was second with a horse which had two splints and straight shoulders. Dragonfly, having fly-jumped with Christo and pulled when ridden by the judges, was third, and Helen Barbersley's Swift was reserve because all the other entries were obviously hopeless.

The jumps in the Handy Hunter competition were the same height as they had been for the jumping: this suited Trappist; he and Henry completed the course without a fault in one minute, thirty seconds. Then they had a long, nerve-racking wait, expecting each competitor in turn to do better than they had. Eric and Christo both made clear rounds, but Eric was nine seconds longer than Henry, and Christo, who had wasted time in the in-and-out, sixteen seconds longer. David, whose mother had made him enter at the last moment, jumped the brush – after two refusals – but was disqualified at the second fence. Juliet exceeded the time limit while trying to shut the gate. Helen and Swift refused three times at the wall. Starshine, despite Paulina's cries of 'hup' and 'coop' and 'over, old lady,' refused to jump the low bar when led in hand. The Ridgeways didn't enter, because their father said they had quite enough trouble to prevent the ponies from stopping in the jumping classes without stopping them on purpose in the Handy Hunter. Alex didn't enter because he couldn't afford more than four events, and he thought that he would have more fun in the races.

So Henry won and, as he cantered round the ring in front of Eric and Christo, he patted Trappist and wondered why all the thrill had gone out of winning.

In the afternoon the day became very hot; the sun burned down upon the showground and there were not nearly enough trees to go round. Henry's head ached and he snapped at his mother when she asked him why he hadn't entered for the Grade C jumping. Deb and Graham Marlowe quarrelled over Golly. They both wanted to canter her up and down the showground. Christo said that she didn't care whether it was incorrect or not, she was going to jump in shirt-sleeves, and she rode into the ring, the first entry in the Grade C jumping. Dragonfly, even more excited since the Handy Hunter, tore round at full speed, bringing down almost every fence with her forelegs. The stewards cursed as they ran out to repair the damage. Helen refused twice at the stile and was disqualified at the gate. Frank Ridgeway made twenty faults with one horse and was disqualified on the other; his father had two refusals and crashed the gate. Mr Galloway fell off and knocked down several fences. A girl of about twenty, called Joan Sumner, made eight faults and when the results were announced she was the winner.

'There, I told you that you should have entered,' said Mrs Thornton to Henry.

David Rice-Greene was staring into space and he didn't hear

his mother's instructions as they waited in the collecting ring for the bending race.

'Now, mind you give Tanzy a good tug at the top post,' said Mrs Rice-Greene. 'I watched the Ridgeways at the show in the Easter holidays and they both gave their ponies a good tug and, whatever people say about them, they do win.'

'O K, Mummy,' answered David, though he hadn't listened to a word of her advice. But Henry, who had overheard the conversation, shuddered with horror and as soon as Mrs Rice-Greene had walked away, he hurried up to David and handed him a card.

'Do come if you can,' he said, putting on his best smile.

'Oh,' said David, collecting his thoughts. 'Thanks a lot.' Henry was glad to see that he read the card before he put it in his pocket.

Alex Turner was standing just outside the collecting ring because Oscar was in a rage and attempted to kick every horse or pony which came near him. Alex wondered vaguely why he entered for gymkhanas; he never jumped a single fence; he was last in every heat; Oscar loathed them and refused to co-operate at all; he supposed that it was really to please his uncle and aunt, who were always worrying about his social life.

Actually, no one ever spoke to him, and he didn't speak to anyone, but as Aunt Esmé and Uncle Geoff never came, it didn't matter. He looked up the other competitors' names and talked about them at dinner.

Alex was very surprised when Henry marched up to him, and saying, 'Look, would you like to join a riding club?' handed him a card.

'Thank you,' said Alex and, when he had read the card, Henry asked:

'Do you think that you will be able to come?'

'Well, the only thing,' said Alex slowly, 'is that Oscar, my pony, isn't a very sociable character, and of course I can't jump or anything.'

'Well, the chief aim of the club is to improve one's riding so your not being able to jump wouldn't matter at all,' answered Henry.

'Then I should like to join very much,' said Alex.

'Good. See you on Thursday.'

'I think it's a wizard idea, Henry,' said Christo, when they met riding towards the collecting ring in preparation for the musical poles. 'I'll certainly join, and I can manage Thursday.'

'That's marvellous,' said Henry. 'I was hoping that you'd be enthusiastic, because you're good at organizing and most of our members are going to be younger than us.'

'I don't suppose that matters,' said Christo. 'Is Elizabeth joining?'

'No, it's not quite in her line,' answered Henry. 'She thinks that if you can stick on you can ride; we're always arguing about it.'

'What about Eric?' asked Christo.

'I'm just going to approach him,' said Henry, 'and there are the Naughtons and Paulina Swindon still to ask. I don't think it's worth bothering about the Ridgeways, do you? They're so very much under "Dad's" influence, and they live so far away.'

'No, I don't think they'd be much use,' answered Christo.

Much to his surprise, Roly Naughton won his heat in the bending. Alex and Oscar had argued at every pole, and Tanzy had galloped David in every direction except the right one. Roly cantered into the collecting ring with a broad grin on his square freckled face. He dismounted and patted Tomahawk's fat roan neck frantically.

'Jolly good, Roly,' shrieked Juliet. 'Now you'll be in the finals.'

Eric won his heat against Frank and Helen. Juliet won hers against Stella and Jannice. Paulina beat Graham Marlowe. A fourth row of posts was erected for the final, which Eric won on Choc-Bloc; Juliet was second, and Roly third. Paulina knocked down a post. While the potatoes were being arranged Henry asked Eric if he would join the riding club.

'You must agree that there ought to be something of the sort round here,' said Henry. 'My idea was that we should ask experts to come down to lecture or instruct us, and that we should run a number of rallies for amusement, with paper-chases and that sort of thing.'

'Yes, it's a good idea on the whole,' Eric answered; 'but, of course, it'll take a good deal of working out. You've got to have a good secretary, and then there are the subscriptions and all that sort of thing to be coped with.'

'Yes. Well, I had thought of Christo Carstairs for secretary,' said Henry; 'but, of course, all that sort of thing has to be discussd at our first meeting.'

'Thursday, isn't it?' asked Eric. 'Yes, I think I shall be able to manage that. Saturday's a hopeless day for me; I'm always showing, and quite often on Wednesdays too.'

Juliet Naughton missed with one of her potatoes and lost the first heat to Eric; as she rode out of the ring Henry handed her a card.

'I wondered whether you would like to join,' he said.

She read it quickly, and replied without a moment's doubt: 'Yes, I should love to join, so would Roly; we've always wished that there was a Pony Club round here.'

There was only Paulina left now, thought Henry; she was still potato-racing, losing her heat to Frank Ridgeway. He stopped her as she came out of the ring.

'A riding club?' said Paulina. 'How wonderful! Of course I should like to join. What fun. Starshine will love it. Thursday, two-thirty. Yes, you can count on me.'

Henry sighed with relief. Now everyone knew except Noel. She was coming tomorrow. 'Come on, Trappist,' he said as Frank, Eric and Helen Barbersley cantered out with their rosettes, and the competitors for the last event – open musical poles – surged into the ring. Everyone had entered for the musical poles and, in consequence, the event seemed endless and the horses which stayed in until last were dripping with sweat. Mr Ridgeway was first, Christo second and Henry third. Oscar disgraced himself by kicking Jannice Barbersley's Swansdown, but fortunately, he didn't hurt her badly. Then the show was over; the shadows of the trees and tents were lengthening across the park; the evening seemed mercifully cool. Henry mounted, and, wending his way through the stream of pedestrians, started for home.

'See you on Thursday,' he called to most of his fellow-competitors.

Helen and Jannice Barbersley hadn't far to ride, for they lived at Trawley Heights, on the extreme outskirts of Waylebury.

'I suppose I was silly to scratch from the jumping,' said Jannice, when they left the main road for a quieter one and were able to ride abreast. 'But, really, I couldn't help it; my old nervousness came back.'

'It's a dreadful waste of money to pay the fees and then not enter,' said Helen: 'I suppose we'd better go to this riding club meeting. I don't like Henry Thornton – he's so stuck up – but if everyone else is joining, we'd better.'

'I'm not sure I want to,' said Jannice, 'they'll always be wanting to jump.'

'Well, Alex Turner and David Rice-Greene can't jump,' remarked Helen, 'and they seem to be joining. That dreadful bad-tempered animal, Oscar, is enough to spoil any riding club. Alex has no control over him at all; he's downright dangerous. Look how he kicked Swansdown; though you ought to have had the sense to keep off his heels. I wonder what the subscription is going to be. *I'm* not paying a lot of money unless it's worth it.'

It didn't take the Barbersleys long to cut out their ponies' plaits and put the tack away in the little lean-to shed adjoining the wooden loose-boxes, which their father had erected when he bought the ponies, two years before. Brown Swift and grey Swansdown drank from their water-trough and, lazily swishing their tails, wandered away to graze. Helen and Jannice left the field and hurried along the road to Byways, their imitation Tudor house. Mrs Barbersley was watching anxiously from an upstairs window. She sighed with relief when her daughters – still neat in white shirts, blue ties, brown crash caps and well-cut coats and jodhs – came in view. She had been worrying about them all day. Now she hurried downstairs as fast as her small fat feet in high-heeled shoes would allow her.

'Hallo, girlies; back already?' she exclaimed brightly, as she opened the door.

'Mummy, look what Helen's won,' said Jannice, pointing at the third and reserve rosettes.

'Oh, what beauties!' exclaimed Mrs Barbersley. 'Well done, Helen – and Swift.'

'We haven't covered our entry fees,' said Helen sourly.

Deborah Marlowe rode Golly home, for it was her turn; Graham and Fanny bicycled beside her.

'Not a single rosette again,' said Graham in disgusted accents. 'I don't know what's the matter with us.'

'Well, you nearly got one in the musical poles,' Deb told him. 'I worked it out, if you'd stayed in five more times you'd have been third.'

'If only Golly would jump,' sighed Fanny. 'I know it's my fault too, but if only she'd just go over the first one for a change.'

'Do you think we can join this riding club?' asked Graham. 'Mummy won't mind, will she?'

'No, of course she won't,' answered Deb.

'I wasn't speaking to you,' said Graham. 'I was asking Fanny.'

'Well, how was I to know?' asked Deb. 'If you don't say Fanny, it might just as well be me.'

'Oh, do shut up,' said Graham. 'What do *you* think, Fanny?'

'Mummy won't mind,' answered Fanny. 'But all the other people ride *miles* better than us, and their ponies jump better than Golly. Then we have to take it in turns to ride and that makes it awkward.'

'Well, the other two could watch,' said Graham, 'and they might teach us to jump, which would be a help.'

'I want to join, even if you don't,' said Deb. 'I want to go to the Manor and jump Golly over the jumps in the field by the stables. I bet I could get her over.'

'I expect they'll say you're too young to join,' Graham told her. 'You oughtn't to belong to the same club as Henry Thornton – he's nearly grown up.'

'Then they'll say you're too young, too,' countered Deb.

'No, they won't,' answered Graham. 'Ten's quite an old age, but eight's definitely babyish.'

'It's not!' shrieked Deb, hitting at him with her hunting-crop.

'It is!' yelled Graham, grabbing at the crop and nearly running his bicycle into Golly.

' 'Tisn't,' shrieked Deb furiously, and she hit her brother a mighty blow with the crop.

'Oh, do stop,' called Fanny in a plaintive voice. But Graham had grabbed the crop and flung it into the middle of a pond which lay at the side of the road.

'Oh, Graham, you shouldn't,' said Fanny, looking hopelessly in the pond.

Fortunately the Marlowes never brooded over their wrongs and so, by the time they reached Vicarage Farm, they were all quite agreeable again. They turned Golly out in the orchard, dumped the tack in a corner of the barn and dashed indoors to tell their parents about the show. All the farm-workers were having the day off, so Mr and Mrs Marlowe had had to stay at home to feed all the animals and milk the cows.

'*Doesn't* Tomahawk look nice with his rosette?' said Juliet
Naughton for the fourth time. 'I think you were jolly good to win
it, Roly; in an under-sixteen class, too.'

'Romeo looks smart, too,' said Roly politely. 'If only we
had a red one. But, still, we shall have seven in the stable
now.'

'Eric Lawson must have hundreds,' said Juliet. 'Oh, dear,' she
went on, 'I do wish I hadn't been so silly in the jumping. I'm glad
there's going to be a riding club,' she said a moment later, 'it's
more fun riding with other people. Besides, we can have a gymkhana. I wonder who'll join. Not Alex; I shouldn't think so anyway – Oscar's such a nuisance. But I expect the Marlowes will –
they live so near.'

'Graham's not bad,' said Roly.

'Look,' said Juliet, as they rounded the last bend in the road,
'there's Mummy at the gate – and Daddy.'

Mr and Mrs Naughton had spent the day at the show, so their
children didn't have to tell them about it. As Juliet dismounted
on the cobbles outside the little brick-and-flint stable, Mrs Naughton began to cut out Romeo's plaits. Mr Naughton was already
unsaddling Tomahawk.

'Give them a drink at the trough,' he said. 'I've got a nice feed
waiting for each of them in the field.'

'I expect you're hungry, too,' said Mrs Naughton. 'I've got a
lovely supper waiting for you indoors.'

Paulina Swindon walked Starshine along the Little Stanton
road wishing that there was someone with whom she could
ride home. None of the horsy children seemed very friendly, she
thought, but perhaps the riding club would change that. Henry
Thornton had disappeared the moment the show had ended; the
Marlowes were very young and they shrieked, so she had trotted
past them. Alex was ahead. He was a funny little boy, she
thought – actually, he was only eighteen months younger than
she. But Alex said 'Good night,' very firmly, when she caught up
with him and, as Oscar was making disagreeable faces, and she
didn't want Starshine kicked, she trotted on. Eric Lawson's trailer
whizzed by; Juliet and Roly turned down the green lane which
was a short-cut to Radney just as she was about to overtake them.
So Paulina rode into Little Stanton alone, wishing that her brother

and sister were with her, but they were both grown up. Aurelia was married, and Julian lived and worked in London.

'I've only you, Starshine,' she said, patting the chestnut neck.

She wished that Starshine was a slightly better jumper; but Mummy always said that it was just as important to be able to lose well as it was to win, and that she didn't want Paulina to become 'show mad'. Anyway they had two rosettes, and it had very nearly been three.

Alex rode home at Oscar's pace, which was very slow indeed. He didn't think about the gymkhana, for he hadn't enjoyed it much; he invented a long story in which Henry Thornton's riding club made Oscar good-tempered, and he became a wonderful jumper. There was time for him to win the jumping at the next year's show before they reached the white gates of The Poplars. Oscar's mane was hogged, so it didn't take long to turn him out. Alex had no oats, so he gave him three carrots and was nearly knocked off his feet, for he was still dreaming and he forgot to dodge Oscar's quarters, which swung round as soon as he had grabbed the carrots. Alex was still dreaming when he entered the house and, when his aunt and uncle, who were his father's younger sister and brother, asked him if he had enjoyed the show, he thought for a moment that they were talking about his imaginary show, the excitement of which had thrust the misery of the real one from his mind.

'Oh, yes,' he answered at last, 'it was great fun. Eric Lawson won nearly everything and Henry Thornton has asked me to join his riding club.'

'That will be nice,' said Aunt Esmé; 'you'll get to know *all* the other teenagers now.'

David Rice-Greene rode round the outskirts of Waylebury and into Trawley with Christo Carstairs. Tanzy had to jog to keep up with Dragonfly's quick walk; David bounced about in the saddle and listened to Christo's conversation with half his attention; the other half observed the shadows of the trees across the road, the faces of the people in the bus queues.

'I must say I think Henry's quite right about the standard of riding,' Christo was saying. 'It seems to get worse each year. But I don't see how this riding club's going to work; it's better to have a grown-up running a thing like that; with all of us about the same age, I should think it'll be one long argument.'

'Oh, I hate arguments,' said David.

'Same here,' agreed Christo; 'but one's got to have them sometimes; one can't just let everything slide.' They rode on in silence for a time, and then Christo said, 'You ought to have your pony's mane pulled. She'd be quite nice looking if she was trimmed up – she might win a prize in a showing class.'

'Do you think she would?' asked David. 'It would please my mother, but I should probably fall off just as the judge was looking.'

'Do you fall off a lot?' asked Christo. And when David admitted that he did, she added kindly, 'All the best riders do in the beginning. Perhaps the riding club will cure you.'

They reached the point where their roads parted. Christo turned right and David rode straight on for Trawley Heights. Tanzy walked her fastest now that she was nearing home. David gazed at the front gardens and, at the end of each road, he decided which he liked best. It was a favourite occupation of his. Later he dismounted stiffly and led Tanzy up the last hill. Barnside, the Rice-Greenes' long, low, white house, was almost in the country. It wasn't a bad house, thought David, but it looked best at the summer half-term when the climbing red roses were in flower. He turned Tanzy out in the orchard and dumped her tack in the toolshed; next time there was a show he would try to plait her mane, he decided.

Eric Lawson was one of the last competitors to leave the showground because he had to unsaddle and box his ponies, but once he was on his way it only took a few minutes to reach home. He travelled with the ponies, sitting on the little wooden tip-seat and holding their head-collar ropes over the cross-bar. It was a very comfortable trailer, but dull on long journeys, for one could only see the back of the car out of the small square window. He looked round at the bridles, swaying gently on their pegs; six rosettes wasn't too bad. He patted both the ponies and thought that they would be worth a lot of money at the end of the summer.

The Paddocks was a well-built modern house and the stables matched it exactly; they were of red brick and the woodwork was painted green. The loose-boxes were ready for the ponies and, while Mrs Lawson cut out Princess's plaits, Eric brushed over Choc-Bloc and Mr Lawson put the car and trailer away. When the ponies were fed and settled for the night Eric nailed the new rosettes beside the others in the saddle-room.

'That blue for the Handy Hunter should have been a red,' said Mr Lawson from the doorway, 'I'm certain that you were faster than Henry Thornton. I wished I had timed you both myself, then I could have made an objection.'

'Well, I don't know,' said Eric; 'but there wasn't much between us anyway.'

'We must begin to look out for a new animal,' said Mrs Lawson. 'We don't want Eric looking like Henry Thornton does on that old grey.'

Chapter 3

HENRY had insisted on riding Evening Echo to Waylebury to meet Noel's train. He had started in good time, but it had taken longer than he had expected to persuade Echo under the railway bridge and up the street to the station and, as he led him on the platform, he saw Noel looking rather forlorn. She was holding Sonnet in one hand and signing forms with the other. Around her were scattered suit-cases, mackintoshes, rugs, tack and grooming kit.

'Hallo, here at last,' said Henry.

'Oh, hallo,' answered Noel in a relieved voice. 'I was just beginning to think I'd come to the wrong station. Is this Echo?' she asked. 'He's huge, but terribly handsome.'

'Sonnet's looking well,' said Henry.

'My pencil, please, miss,' said the porter, who had observed that Noel was pocketing it absent-mindedly.

'I thought we could ride home,' said Henry. 'My mother's going to collect all your luggage. You seem to have brought enough for an expedition to the Antarctic.'

'Well, five weeks is a long time,' said Noel, 'though I'm sure you'll all be fed up with me after one. However, you can tell me if you are and I'll go and stay with Aunt Irene.'

' 'Ere, we must get this 'orse off the platform,' said the porter in a bored voice. 'We'll 'ave the station-master complaining.'

'OK,' said Noel, grabbing the bridle and tangling her legs in the reins.

'I'll hold her,' said Henry, 'while you put the saddle on.'

At last everything was organized; Noel and Henry mounted and rode out of the station and down the street. Sonnet was very excited; she pranced along with pricked ears, but Echo was quieter now that he had a companion. They rode in single file and conversation consisted of Henry shouting rude remarks about the town and its gasworks, until they reached the country roads and were able to ride abreast.

Noel couldn't think of anything to say to Henry at first; except for a day's hunting at Christmas, she had not seen him since the summer holidays the year before when they had both stayed at Folly Court with the Holbrookes. They had written to each other several times, and Henry had sent all the West Barsetshire people Christmas cards, but now, riding along on Echo, he looked much older, taller and more superior than Noel remembered him and she felt sure that he was wishing that he hadn't invited her to stay.

However, Henry began to talk; he told her about the Waylebury show and how badly everyone had ridden, about the riding club and how she was to help run it, about Echo and how his schooling always seemed to make him worse instead of better.

As they neared Radney, Noel told Henry about the Brampton show and how Susan Barington-Brown had won the pony class, and there had been six clear rounds in the juvenile jumping. They had jumped off four times and in the end, John Manners had won; Sonnet had been second.

Then Henry said, 'Here we are,' and turned up the drive. The house, part ancient monastery, part Tudor manor, stood before them, a warm grey against the bright green of the hill which rose behind it.

'What a lovely house,' said Noel.

'It's damn draughty in winter,' answered Henry.

They rode through the shrubberies to the stables where Finch was waiting for them. He seemed pleased to have Sonnet to stay.

'Another grey,' he said; 'but she's a nice little thing.' He left Henry to deal with Echo and helped Noel. 'I thought you'd like to 'ave 'er stabled,' he said, 'what with the riding club and all this dressage stuff, they need to be fit. Not that Echo couldn't do with more work.' Noel liked Finch; she was still talking to him when Henry appeared to say that they were already half an hour late for tea.

The drawing-room at Radney Manor was long and low, and there was a magnificent view of the famous Radney oaks from its mullioned windows. Mrs Thornton, who was pouring tea from a silver teapot into tiny cups and talking to a visitor, rose to greet Noel. She was tall and rather solid; her greying hair was drawn back smoothly into a loose knot; her features were good except that her mouth was on the small side and her chin a little too decided.

'How do you do?' she said, shaking hands with Noel. 'It's so nice of you to come and stay with us; Henry's told me all about you. Did you have a terrible journey cooped up in that dreadful truck? It seemed so unnecessary for you to travel with the horse. I suppose you took some sandwiches for lunch.'

'How do you do?' answered Noel as soon as Mrs Thornton paused for breath. 'I had a very pleasant journey, thank you, and lots of sandwiches.'

Mrs Thornton cross-questioned Noel on a variety of subects for several minutes, without, apparently, listening to her answers, and then she began to tell Mrs Phipps – the visitor – about her idea for the revival of old English crafts in village homes. At intervals, usually when Mrs Phipps was speaking to her, she turned and said, 'Don't flop so, Henry, dear,' or, 'Henry, do give poor Noel something to eat.'

When they had finished drinking the tepid tea and eating cucumber sandwiches and the very elderly cake, Henry showed Noel all the objects of interest in the room. Engravings after Reynolds, seventeenth-century miniatures and a shoe worn and left behind by Queen Elizabeth, when she had stayed at the Manor. Then he announced that they were going to take the dogs for a walk. The sleeping dogs – Roger the labrador, Rufus the cocker spaniel and Ruddy the young bull terrier – immediately woke and became wild with excitement.

'Shall we go to the stables first and make sure Sonnet's all right?' Henry shouted to be heard above the frantic barking.

On Wednesday Noel and Henry spent most of the morning schooling. Sonnet was going well and Noel felt very pleased with her; Finch was giving her a good many oats and she was just beginning to get fit again after her term-time rest; next week, Noel planned, she would teach her the half-pass at the canter. Echo was not in an obliging mood and, after he had given one of what Henry called his displays – which consisted of bucking, rearing and jumping into the air, alternately, for about five minutes – Noel found herself stationed in the middle of the school being badgered for advice.

'You see,' said Henry, pulling up and pushing his fair hair out of his eyes after a particularly strenuous bout of bucking and napping, 'I've never given in to him, and yet he persists in behaving like this. Elizabeth says that I've soured him with too much schooling, but hacking him for a week doesn't make any difference, nor does a term-time holiday of six weeks; besides, he's always done it, and his previous owner had made no attempt to school him.'

'Well,' said Noel, rather dubiously, 'I think I know what I'd do with him if he were mine, but I'm probably quite wrong, and I don't suppose you'll agree, but if he belonged to me, I'd put him back in a snaffle.'

'A snaffle; but I'm trying to teach him collection,' objected Henry.

'But he's not ready for collection. He's not on the bit yet,' argued Noel. 'You can't say that he goes forward freely with a steady head carriage and active hind legs.'

'No, I suppose I can't,' agreed Henry ruefully. 'All right, back to the beginning. Look, I thought we could go for a hack this afternoon. Echo needs masses of work and if Sonnet's done enough, you could try Trappist.'

Noel enjoyed riding Trappist who was well-schooled and sensible, but she found Echo's behaviour maddening. He kicked at cars, was driven to crazy fits of bucking by the sight of combine harvesters and shot off at a gallop whenever there was the smallest rustle in a hedge. 'He's always like this,' explained Henry rather breathlessly after a particularly wild fit of bucking. 'Still, he's no more uncontrollable in a snaffle.'

. Then they lost Ruddy and had to ride back to a downland rabbit warren where they found him digging.

'The Thornton animals are behaving atrociously,' said Henry in depressed tones. 'You'll end up regretting that you didn't go to Aunt Irene's.'

Noel denied this firmly, but when they arrived at the house and found Mrs Thornton fuming because they were three-quarters of an hour late for tea she began to feel that there might be some truth in it. However, Henry's father, a small, grey-haired peaceable man, had just returned from a business trip, and he calmed everyone and showed Noel all the interesting objects in the house, includung the ones Henry had showed her the day before.

On Thursday morning Henry had another argument with his mother, this time over the lemon squash and cake for the riding club members, and it was only resolved by Elizabeth offering to drive Henry and Noel to Waylebury to buy the cake. As soon as they got back they rushed to prepare the field for the handicap jumping competition, which they proposed to hold when the dull part of the meeting was over. When Henry saw the field he gave a cry of horror.

'Oh, heavens,' he said. 'We're never going to be ready in time, that's obvious. The jumps look absolutely squalid; I ought to have white-washed them. Still, I bet no one turns up and the whole meeting is a ghastly fiasco.'

'Oh, don't be so depressing,' said Noel, picking up a prostrate hurdle; 'you're giving me the needle.'

'The brush fence looks as though rats had been gnawing it,' observed Henry in dissatisfied accents.

Fortunately Finch appeared at that moment and instantly took charge. He found the mallet and set Henry to work knocking in posts; he told Noel where to find a hammer and nails with which to mend the wall, and then hurried away in search of pea-sticks for the brush. He returned with Sid, the gardener, a wheelbarrow piled with pea-sticks and two pairs of hedge clippers. In ten minutes the brush was transformed, Noel had mended the wall and Henry had moved and re-erected the stile. Finch knocked in the triple posts because he said that Henry was slow and always taking rests. Sid made a jump out of bundles of pea-sticks for the people whose horses wouldn't jump the brush. Noel collected a bar and two petrol cans and made an alternative jump to the wall. Finch and Henry fixed the gate and arranged a bar, which could take its place for the smaller ponies; they knocked in the hurdles and the course was ready.

Henry looked round. 'I wish we had some parallels,' he said; 'but still, it all looks very professional now. Thanks awfully,' he said to Finch and Sid. 'Without you such a transformation would have been impossible and the riding club people would have despised Radney Manor for ever.' Sid said, 'You're welcome,' and Finch, 'Another time you let us know a bit earlier, then we can do the job properly. It's daft the way you leave everything to the last minute.'

'Well, I've only been home from school five days,' protested Henry, 'and look what I've had to do in that time, with the horse show and Noel coming, and all that wretched typing. It isn't as though I'm a practical or efficient character.'

'No, you're not, and that's a fact,' said Finch, winking at Noel.

At two-fifteen all the prospective members were converging on Radney Manor. Eric had decided to hack over on Princess; he rode along beside Paulina telling her about the horse show in which he had competed the day before. He told her of his own successes, insisting, modestly, that the competition had been poor, and of the two objections which his father had had to make.

Paulina was a good listener; she gazed into your face, gave you all her attention and made the right noises – noises which indicated delight, disgust or disappointment – at the appropriate moment.

'What bad luck,' she murmured when Eric had finished speaking and, as they turned up the Radney Manor drive, she began to relate a similar experience of her own.

Christo Carstairs had the longest way to ride, but Dragonfly's quick walk soon covered the dull roads of Trawley and brought her out into the rich summer countryside. It was the third fine day in succession. The last of the hay was carried; the corn was turning gold. Of all the year, thought Christo, summer was the time she liked best. It was the season for riding, tennis and swimming – her three favourite pastimes.

When she turned the corner by the pond she could see David Rice-Greene ahead; he was allowing Tanzy to dawdle along; an odd boy, thought Christo, he didn't compare very well with

Gerry and Bill; they were real boys – always up to something. It was a pity that they didn't like riding. But this tall, pale, thin David didn't look as though he could say boo to a goose.

'Hallo,' she said, catching up with him. 'Isn't it a lovely day? You'll have to hurry up, you know,' she added, 'or you'll be late.'

David, who had been thinking that all ripening corn wasn't golden, for the spangled oats looked more like silver, was rather annoyed at having his thoughts interrupted.

'I shan't be any later than you,' he replied, 'and, anyway, I don't suppose that anyone will notice if I am.'

It was Fanny Marlowe's turn for first ride, and she wasn't at all pleased, because the Vicarage Farm was only a mile and a half from Radney Manor, and the lane was hard at this time of year, so there were no canters. Graham and Deb, who had decided that the distance was too short to need bicycles, walked or ran beside her.

'It's a waste of a turn,' grumbled Fanny every few moments until Graham said:

'Well, it's my turn to ride back, so it's only Deb who'll score, and she's not allowed to hunt.'

'Next season I shall be,' said Deb.

'I wonder if there'll be jumping,' said Fanny. 'Please try, Golly, if there is.'

'Oh, I hope there will be. Oh, there must be,' shrieked Deb. 'I'm sure I shall get Golly over.'

Helen and Jannice were feeling much too hot and rather disagreeable. They always wore vests, long-sleeved shirts and riding-coats even in the height of summer, so hot days were no pleasure to them.

'I'm sure I shall be made to jump,' wailed Jannice, who was becoming more apprehensive the nearer they drew to Radney Manor. 'Oh, I do wish that you hadn't made me come.'

'Well, go home, then,' said Helen. 'I don't care. It's a waste of a subscription for you to join anyway.'

'All right,' said Jannice tearfully. 'I will.' And she tugged Swansdown round and tried to ride homewards, but Swansdown wouldn't go; she swung round and rejoined Swift at a trot. 'Oh dear,' wailed Jannice, turning white with terror and holding on to the pommel of her saddle. 'She won't go.'

'Kick her,' advised Helen in exasperated accents. 'Oh, well, you'd better come on, then. You're sure to fall off and then I shall get the blame.'

To Alex's annoyance he had met the Naughtons just outside his gate, and he had to ride the half-mile to Radney Manor with them. Juliet told him all about her end-of-term feast, about the party to which she had been the day before and the difficulty they had had to catch Tomahawk that morning. At intervals she turned in her saddle to make signals and warning faces at Roly, who was inclined to ride too near Oscar's heels.

'You seem to lead a very busy life,' said Alex, when there was a pause in the conversation.

'Oh, Roly and I are very lucky,' replied Juliet, and she decided to invite Alex to her next party, for he didn't seem to have much fun.

Henry was receiving the prospective members at the top of the drive and directing them to the field. Noel was sitting on the field gate and listening to their remarks as they rode in.

Eric borrowed a loose-box for Princess, who wouldn't tie up, and then Helen and Paulina wanted stables for their ponies too, but Henry was very firm. He said that if he dirtied too many stables he would have Finch after him, and any horse that would tie up was to be tied to the railings in the shade of the fir plantation. He provided halters for all the people who had forgotten to bring them, and Alex tied Oscar in a secluded corner so that he wouldn't kick anyone.

Everyone agreed that the fir plantation would be much the coolest place to hold a meeting, and so they climbed the rails and pushed their way through to a little clearing. The small people, Roly and the younger Marlowes, crawled about under the trees, while their elders sat or sprawled in the clearing. They were glad of the gloomy light after the glare of the sun.

'I love the smell of pine needles,' said Noel, sniffing loudly.

'Do firs have pine needles?' asked Eric in a voice which implied correction.

David, who was lying on his stomach, answered, 'I don't see why not. After all, pines have fir cones.'

'Perhaps they ought to be called pine cones,' suggested Christo.

'Pineapples,' said Roly.

'Oh, yes, they're jolly good. I like the kind in tins best,' said Graham.

'Oh, shut up,' said Deb. 'You're making my mouth water.'

'Ladies and gentlemen,' said Henry loudly, 'we are not here to discuss nature or food, but a riding club. The first thing to decide is, do we want a riding club? Will those in favour yell, aye; those against, no.'

There was a loud chorus of ayes, people like Deb and Roly seizing the opportunity to make as much noise as possible, and no noes.

'That seems fairly conclusive,' observed Henry. 'Now, I think that the first aim of the club should be to improve the standard of horsemanship in this district. Do you agree?'

'I should like to say something about that,' said Eric, looking round at the other members and then at the ground. 'You see, though I agree that we ought to try to improve people's riding, I can't see any point in having a club unless we get some fun out of it. Even the people who are learning need some fun or they'll get fed up, and then there are the people who'll never be much good – it's not their fault – one can't do much about them, for you can't get away from the fact that horsemen are born, not made.'

'Hear, hear. I quite agree,' cried Paulina.

Noel was sitting up and obviously preparing for speech.

Henry grinned at her and began hastily, 'I think Eric is going ahead rather fast,' he said. 'He's started talking about aim number two, but I gather that he agrees with our first aim. Does everyone else?'

There was a murmur of yes, and Henry in a brisk voice said, 'Right. Now, aim two. Eric has suggested that it shall be to provide amusement for members, presumably in the form of games, paper-chases, mock hunts, etc. Has anyone anything to say?'

'Let's have a gymkhana,' said Juliet without hesitation.

'Yes,' shrieked Deb Marlowe. 'A gymkhana with jumping for people under ten.'

'Oh, shush, Deb,' said Fanny.

'No shushing, please,' said Henry. 'Freedom of speech must be preserved.'

'Sorry,' replied Fanny meekly.

'Lots and lots of competitions and no beastly dull old showing classes,' bawled Roly.

'But, Roly –' began Juliet.

'There *must* be jumping,' interrupted Deb.

'People can't just arrange everything to suit themselves,' objected Eric.

'How much would the entry fees be?' asked Helen.

'Order, order,' shouted Henry. 'The gymkhana or horse show cannot be discussed today. If one of our aims is to hold an annual show a special sub-committee must be elected to arrange the details. The point is, shall the holding of a show be our third aim?'

'Yes,' said everyone, but the Marlowes and Naughtons made the most noise.

'Would anyone like to suggest a fourth aim?' asked Henry.

There was a pause and then Paulina said, 'I think we ought to have some wider aim. Something a little more unselfish and worthwhile. What about preventing cruelty to animals or something of that sort?'

Henry answered, 'I think that the R.S.P.C.A. and the Boy Scouts deal very adequately with those points.'

Noel said, in a very indignant voice, 'Surely raising the standard of horsemanship is a worthwhile aim?'

'Any more views?' asked Henry. 'Paulina, would you like to propose a rather more concrete aim?'

'No,' she replied in rather martyred accents, 'I just thought – but since you don't agree – I mean it doesn't matter a bit.'

'Well, if no one has any more aims the next thing to discuss is the name. I called it the Radney Riding Club because I thought that probably this field would be the centre of club activity, and it sounded well. But what do you all think?'

'A very good name,' said Christo.

'I like it,' answered Noel.

'O K by me,' said David.

'And me,' added Alex.

'I think that Radney confines us to a very narrow radius,' objected Eric.

'I think it's a dull name,' said Paulina. 'Couldn't we have something that explained our aims?'

'Any suggestions?' asked Henry.

'The Rum Riding Club,' said Roly, and then collapsed in a fit of giggles on top of Graham. They began to scuffle and in a moment Deb had joined in.

'Deb, Graham,' called Fanny plaintively; 'do stop.' Juliet laughed indulgently. Eric looked annoyed and Henry shouted: 'Order, order.'

As the scufflers sat up, he added, 'Though we do not expect the younger members of this club to behave with all the dignity and decorum of their elders, we do think they might make some attempt to control their animal spirits.'

'Hear, hear, hear,' said Christo.

'Boo,' said Roly.

'Shut up, Roly,' said Juliet.

'Well, if no one can suggest another name; those in favour of calling it the Radney Riding Club?' asked Henry.

Everyone except Eric and Paulina was in favour, and so the club was named. Henry rushed through the election of the club officers. He was chosen as chairman, Christo as secretary and Eric as treasurer. Then they discussed subscriptions for ages. Helen wanted them low and Eric, high. In the end Christo suggested a compromise; two and sixpence from that day to Christmas and then another meeting to discuss what they should be for the following year. This was agreed upon, and then they began to talk about the first rally; it was to be an instructive one. The question was, whom should they invite to instruct them? Henry and Noel grumbled about the inconsiderate way in which Major Holbrooke had gone abroad for the summer holidays. Paulina suggested that they should ask the local vet to give them a talk. Eric volunteered to persuade his father to write to a Colonel Sanderson, who, he said, was the Master of the Fording and Benlake Harriers, did a lot of judging and certainly knew his stuff.

Henry and Noel had never heard of him, but Paulina said that she thought that she had and, as no one else could suggest another expert, it was settled that Eric should persuade his father to write, that night if possible.

'Hurray,' said Henry. 'That's the end of the meeting. To horse!'

There was a wild stampede to the railings and stables, for almost everyone was longing to try the jumps.

'I thought,' said Henry, when they were all mounted and ready, 'that we would have a handicap jumping competition. The jumps will be below two feet for the ponies which haven't won a prize for jumping and then at three feet three for horses, and the ponies which have won prizes. They're three feet three now. Who'd like to go first?'

'I'll go if no one else wants to,' said Eric. 'But don't you think the fences should be a little higher? We don't want too much jumping off.'

'Well, I'm not going to do a clear round; you can count on that, I promise you,' said Paulina.

'Nor me,' added Juliet.

'I don't think there'll be many,' said Henry. 'Not unless everyone's jumping better than they did at Waylebury.'

'Oh, all right. I'll go, then,' said Eric. He cantered a circle and then rode at the first jump. As Princess flew over Henry said:

'He'll make a clear round.' And Eric did. Nobody seemed to want to jump next, so Henry said that he would and that a stretcher party had better prepare. But Echo liked jumping. He refused the brush fence because he had been playing up and hadn't noticed it, but after that he cleared everything, except the stile, though he was taking off all over the place and bucking whenever he thought that he had jumped particularly well.

'Gosh,' said Roly. 'I wish Tomahawk would do that.'

'You wouldn't stay on if he did,' observed Juliet. 'I don't know how Henry does.'

'Oh, they're not much, really,' said Eric. 'It's the short-backed cobs like Choc-Bloc who really know how to put you down.'

'Come on, Noel,' said Henry, when he rejoined the others, 'you're next.'

'Oh, dear, I've got terrible needle,' said Noel.

'Nonsense,' said Henry firmly.

Noel and Sonnet jumped a clear round; they were fast but very quiet. Eric looked rather surprised.

'That's a jolly good pony. Whom did Noel get her from?' he asked Henry.

'She was given to her as a prize,' explained Henry. 'She was very thin and completely green, and Noel schooled her.'

'Well, she hasn't done it too badly,' said Eric. 'I'm all for school-ing one's own horses. Of course Choc-Bloc was almost unrideable when my father bought him – he used to put me down, I can tell you – and Princess was very gassy and hot.'

'Christo, will you jump next?' asked Henry.

Dragonfly made her usual destructive round. Completely out of control, she crashed almost every fence with her forelegs to the annoyance of David, Alex and Deb, who were acting as stewards.

'I'm the person who needs the instructive rally,' said Christo, as she rode back. 'Honestly, I haven't an ounce of control over this animal – she's completely scatty.'

'You ought to hold her back longer,' advised Eric.

'What about tightening your martingale?' suggested Paulina.

'You're next, Paulina,' said Henry.

Paulina rode Starshine at the brush fence, but, as she drew near, she stopped using her legs and merely cried 'hup'. Starshine refused twice, then jumped it. She knocked down the stile and was disqualified for running out at the wall.

'You bad old girl,' said Paulina, patting her and riding back with a sporting smile on her lips. 'She's a bit off colour today,' Paulina explained. Juliet and Romeo were also disqualified; they ran out at the gate, the wall and the triple.

'There ought to be wings,' complained Paulina to Juliet. 'It's too much to expect hunters to jump these narrow fences in cold blood.'

'Well, the others managed to,' answered Juliet.

'Yes, but they're Henry's jumps; Noel has probably practised over them, and Eric's ponies are trained show-jumpers. Starshine is primarily a hunter; she just doesn't understand narrow fences like these.'

'Now for the smaller ponies,' Henry was saying as he began to put the jumps down.

'Thank you,' said Helen in offended accents. 'I should like to point out that Swift is the third tallest horse here and he *has* won prizes.'

'Oh, hallo. Haven't you been yet? I'm terribly sorry; I forgot all about you,' said Henry.

'So I see,' said Helen in cold tones.

Henry hastily restored the jump, which he had altered, to its original height.

'O K,' he said, 'all set; you can carry on now.'

'Very well,' replied Helen, and rode towards the first jump. But Swift was reluctant to compete; with a small buck and a half-rear he turned and carried Helen back to the other horses. She tried again. 'Get on,' she said, kicking him and jerking at his mouth, but as soon as he began to play up her hands would rest on his neck and her legs would do nothing. She became red in the face and cross as well as nervous. At last Henry offered to ride Swift.

'I don't suppose I can get him to jump,' he said; 'but I'll have a shot if you like.'

'Oh, very well; if you want to,' answered Helen ungraciously. 'But he's just playing me up, that's all; he usually jumps all right.'

Henry mounted. He crossed the stirrups, to save altering them, and gave Swift the aid to go forward. Swift moved off and then tried to swing round, but Henry's legs were ready for him; they pushed him forward and, after one small defiant buck, the little horse gave in and jumped round the course, only bringing down the stile. Roly, Graham and Deb clapped.

'Well done,' cried Paulina.

'How does he do it?' asked Juliet.

'Legs, gentlemen, legs,' murmured Noel, and Eric remarked: 'Oh, a horse always knows when his rider means business.'

Noel, Christo and Juliet began to alter the jumps.

'I'm going to ask Henry to jump Dragonfly afterwards,' Christo told Noel. 'He might have a good effect on her too, but I think that she's just scatty.'

'It's worth trying,' agreed Noel, wishing that she were a famous equitation expert, who could air her opinions instead of having to listen to other people making silly remarks in silence. You're getting terribly conceited, she told herself.

The small ponies jumped even worse than the bigger ones. Tanzy galloped David past the first jump three times. Oscar refused to contemplate jumping, despite Alex's flapping legs and the loan of Eric's whip. Jannice held Swansdown on a short tight rein and refused to let her jump; then, at her third attempt, everyone shouted at her to let the reins go. She did. Swansdown jumped, and Jannice fell off and burst into tears. Paulina and Juliet rushed to her rescue. Helen said, 'Shut up, you little fool,' in an unsympathetic voice. Everyone else looked slightly embarrassed.

Fanny Marlowe, who jumped Golly first, persuaded her over the brush, after two refusals, but was disqualified at the next jump. Graham, who jumped second, accomplished two jumps and was disqualified at the third fence, and Deb, who rode Golly last, jumped three fences. To everyone's surprise Roly completed the course, but he fell off twice, ran out twice, knocked down the stile and jagged Tomahawk's mouth over nearly every fence. Everyone told Juliet that he ought to have a neck-strap, for Tomahawk's mane was hogged, so he had nothing to hold on by, except the reins.

Then Henry announced the results. 'Noel and Eric to jump off,' he said. 'The rest of us are too bad to bother about.'

Noel and Eric each jumped another clear round when the fences were raised; then they jumped again with the fences higher still, and each had four faults at the stile. Christo suggested that they should try the stile again, and this time they both cleared it.

'Well, now what do you want to do?' asked Henry.

'I don't mind,' said Eric. 'I mean, if Noel wants to go on I will, but I must say that I think that the ground's none too good, and I am going to a show on Saturday, so I don't want to get Princess stale.'

'O K,' said Noel. 'Let's stop. Sonnet's about reached her limit, and I don't want to overface her.'

'Oh,' groaned Roly in dissatisfied accents. 'I wanted to see them jump six feet.'

'I wonder if Golly could jump those,' said Deb.

'Of course not, you little goose,' Paulina answered her.

'Look,' said Henry, 'I think that, if everyone has time, the winners might put their horses in the stables, and then we'll try to improve the also-rans. Any objections?'

'Good idea,' answered Christo.

So Noel and Eric put their mounts away and when they returned on foot, they found that the jumps were back at their first height.

'You two are to stand in the middle and give helpful advice,' said Henry. 'I'm the first victim.'

This time Echo jumped the brush fence without hesitation, but, once again, he brought down the stile.

'He takes off too near,' said Noel.

'Push him a bit harder,' advised Eric.

Henry tried again, but the pushing only made Echo put in

more short strides and he jumped even worse than before.

'Your timing's not quite right,' said Eric. 'I'll shout on the take-off next time.' But next time was no better.

'What do you think, Noel?' asked Henry.

'Well, I should try a bar on the ground in front to show him where to take off,' said Noel rather diffidently. 'That's what the Major does anyway.'

'O K,' said Henry. They placed a bar about three feet in front of the stile and when Henry rode at it again, Echo took off before the bar and cleared the stile easily.

'Hurray,' said Henry, jumping off and patting him. 'I'll take him in now. Wait for me before you begin, Christo; I won't be a sec.' And he ran off with Echo bucking and leaping about behind him. Finch was watching over the gate, so he took Echo, and Henry was soon back.

'Stewards, get ready,' said Christo as she rode at the first fence.

'Hold her back more,' shouted Eric as Dragonfly hurled herself over, clearing the brush fence by half an inch. But the more Christo tried to hold her back, the hotter and more excitable Dragonfly became. She cantered higher and higher into the air; she fly-jumped and finally she wrenched the reins from Christo's hands and flung herself at the fence, bringing it down with her forelegs.

'You'll have to hold her back somehow,' said Eric; 'try sawing at her mouth. That mare needs a gag,' he added to Henry and Noel.

'Sawing at her mouth won't do any good,' said Noel, stung to action. 'You'll only hot her up more than ever.'

'Here, Henry, you see what you can do,' said Christo, dismounting.

Henry mounted, saying that he hadn't an idea what to do and that he was obviously going to fall off.

'Well, at least I shall see what she does,' said Christo. 'Normally, I haven't a clue.'

At first Henry tried to make Dragonfly approach the fences more slowly, but with the same lack of result as Christo. Then he tried circling her in front of the fence, but she only became more and more excitable and threw her head about. After Dragonfly had crashed the jump six times, he pulled up, and asked:

'Any suggestions?'

'I've told you mine,' said Eric. 'A gag, and you may as well try one of those combined running and standing martingales as well.'

'She'll look like a saddler's shop,' objected Christo.

'I should give up trying to show-jump her; she obviously hasn't the temperament,' advised Paulina.

'I should give her more work; tire her out, then she'll go more quietly,' said Helen.

'Nonsense,' said Henry. 'A well-bred horse can't be quietened by work unless you underfeed him. You can work off overfreshness, but not a temperament. Look at the way high-couraged horses come home after a day's hunting.'

'I don't think she's ready to jump yet,' said Noel. 'She hasn't learned to accept her bit. You can't control her because one moment she's in front of it and the next she's behind it.'

'Schooling in a snaffle and a drop noseband,' said Henry, grinning at Noel, 'the cure of all ills.'

'I doubt whether you could control her in one out hacking,' said Noel; 'but for schooling at the walk and trot—'

'But I want to jump her in the shows these holidays,' protested Christo.

'Try her in a gag,' said Eric.

'Christo, you've had two sets of advice; follow which you will. It should be an interesting experiment,' said Henry. 'Come on, Paulina,' he added, 'you're the next victim.'

There was no argument over Paulina; it was obvious to all that she used her legs until she drew near to the fence and then, at the very moment when her pony should have increased her speed, Paulina's legs stopped working and she cried 'hup' hopefully instead. They pointed this out to her in vain and at last Eric rode Starshine, who promptly jumped every fence with ease.

When it was Helen's turn she said that Swift had jumped enough and, when Christo tried to persuade her to have a try, she replied stiffly that she would rather not.

Juliet attended carefully to the advice that was given her. Eric said that she was like Paulina and didn't use her legs enough. Henry pointed out that reins as well as legs were necessary to keep Romeo straight. Noel thought that she leaned forward and gave Romeo his head too early – a couple of strides before the take-off, instead of on the take-off – and that was how he managed to run out. Christo said that her reins were yards too loose.

At last Juliet jumped the course with only one run out – at the wall – and Romeo was patted and allowed to stop.

The schooling of the small ponies and their riders was much less successful. Roly, provided with a neckstrap, was the only person who showed any improvement at all. At last, tired of the sight of weak riders and refusing ponies, they turned off the owners. Eric mounted Oscar, Noel Golly. Alex, who had shown some signs of using his legs, was given Tanzy and Fanny Marlowe was told to try Swansdown. Noel persuaded Golly to jump every-thing and then changed to Swansdown while Henry gave Graham a lesson on Golly. Eric, looking extremely hot, said that it was all he could do to make Oscar jump, that he wasn't surprised Alex couldn't, and that he had never ridden a pony with less idea of jumping in his life, and was Alex sure that he wasn't a mule? – he looked and behaved like one. Alex only answered, 'Poor Oscar.' He had managed to jump everything on Tanzy, and he felt quite pleased with himself, because Henry had only told him to keep his heels down and his knees in. If only Oscar were more agreeable, he thought, I wouldn't mind him not being able to jump. He patted Oscar's neck, but as usual was rewarded with a frightful face and a snap at his hand.

'I never knew Tanzy could jump like that,' said David enthusi-astically, as he patted her after jumping round the course with only one run out. 'That was super.'

'She's a good little jumper,' said Noel, returning Swansdown to Jannice, 'and a very nice ride. You get up now and have a try.'

'Oh, no, thank you; I'd rather not,' answered Jannice quickly. 'You see, I'm nervous – I always have been, though I'm getting over it a little now.'

'Well, then, there's no need to jump at all,' said Noel. 'I should give it up and practise other things like reining-back, and the turn on the forehand and riding without stirrups until you're not nervous at all. There's no reason why you should jump; only you shouldn't ride Swansdown at jumps until you're perfectly certain that you want to go over.'

'Oh, but I can jump,' said Jannice. 'I've jumped three feet.'

'Well, you shouldn't have jumped three feet,' said Noel rather indignantly. 'You probably jagged your pony's mouth. You oughtn't to jump higher than one foot till you've improved.'

'That's everyone, then,' said Henry with relief, when he heard that Jannice didn't want to jump. 'What an afternoon.'

'It's not fair,' said Deb's voice rising above the general conversation and gradually breaking into a wail. 'It's not fair. Fanny's had eleven jumps and Graham's had nine, and I've only had seven.'

'Oh, shush, Deb,' said Fanny hastily. 'Don't make such a noise; you can have some extra jumps next time.'

'I don't want them next time,' yelled Deb, louder than before. ' 'Tisn't fair; I want them now.'

'Spoilt brat,' said Eric.

'Poor little thing,' said Paulina. 'Let's give her another one or two.'

'No fear' said Christo. 'That'll simply encourage her.'

'Order, order,' said Henry. 'Today's rally, as already announced, is over. The ponies have had quite enough, and if Miss What's-her-name Marlowe doesn't like the way the club is run she can resign. Those who want lemon squash, follow me.'

In the cool of the evening, when all the lemon squash and cakes had been devoured, and the slanting sun had turned the grey stone of Radney Manor to warm gold, the riding club members mounted and rode homewards.

'Good-bye and thank you,' they called, and Eric said, 'I'll let you know about Sanderson.'

The sound of hoofs, scrunching down the drive and clattering on the road, gradually died away into the distance. The Radney oaks and their hill-top were an island of green and gold in the blaze of the evening sun and in the valley, between the Manor and the oaks, the dipping fields were already dim and shadowed. From the spinney across the road came the contented murmur of wood-pigeons. Henry and Noel leaned on the stable doors and spoke to their munching horses, and then they wandered leisurely to the house.

Chapter 4

HENRY and Noel, tired of discussing the characters and faults of
the other members of the Radney Riding Club, were reading in
the drawing-room after dinner when Eric Lawson rang up. Henry
ran to answer the telephone, which was downstairs in the hall,
and Noel was left with his parents.

Mrs Thornton was looking at the *Queen*, and at intervals she
interrupted everyone else's reading with a cry of 'Oh, here's a
photo of Annabel (or Mrs Hope Dunster or Colonel Macleod). What
a sight! Whatever possessed her? Just look at this terrible outfit.'

Mr Thornton merely grunted or murmured, 'Yes, dear, Macleod
has grown fat, poor fellow,' without taking his eyes from his
book; but Noel, being a visitor, felt compelled to rise and take an
interest. She soon became tired of agreeing. 'Yes, it's dreadful;
what a nice dog, though. Yes, it's a perfectly terrible hat.'

At last Henry returned. 'Eric's more efficient than I thought,' he
said. 'He persuaded his father to telephone Sanderson and he's
going to come on Monday. It was fearsome cheek to ask him at
such short notice, but Eric said that he didn't mind a bit. He's
going to lunch with the Lawsons and come over here at two-
fifteen.'

'Now, I suppose we must start ringing up the members,' said
Noel.

'Certainly not,' answered Henry. 'That's Christo's job, and I've
already telephoned her and told her so.'

On Friday it poured with rain. Despite Mrs Thornton's asser-
tions that it was quite unnecessary for them to do so, Noel and
Henry took Sonnet and Echo for a ride. Echo was even sillier
than usual. He kicked at cars, shied at squirrels, refused to
go through puddles and bumped into Sonnet at every possible
opportunity. The rain had found its way through Henry's mackintosh and down Noel's back long before they turned homewards. The reins were wet and slippery, their gloves were soaked
and, with the wind towards them as they took the green lane
from Little Stanton, the rain lashed their faces and made the
horses carry their heads between their forelegs. In spite of the

discomfort Noel enjoyed herself; there was something exhilarating about the feel of the rain on her face; she felt that she wanted to gallop into the wind alone with Sonnet; it was the sort of day on which you want to gallop for ever and ever.

Saturday, in contrast, dawned fair and dry. Small white clouds scudded gaily across a blue sky and a brisk breeze dried up the puddles. Most of the Radney Riding Club members seized the opportunity to school their ponies. David Rice-Greene, who had exaggerated the height of the fences he and Tanzy had jumped on Thursday until his mother refused to believe that he had jumped at all, invited her to watch him in the orchard. His jumps, made out of bean-poles and hoes propped up on buckets, were very flimsy and Tanzy refused to treat them seriously; she dragged her legs through them, making no attempt to jump. Mrs Rice-Greene gave scornful laughs each time this happened and David, becoming rather red in the face and cross, finally hit Tanzy as hard as he could. She shot straight into a gallop and, with her head in the air and her mouth open, tore twice round the orchard before sweeping David off under the branches of a low apple tree.

'Oh, you're impossible, David,' grumbled Mrs Rice-Greene. 'Why didn't you stop her? Now you've scratched your face and torn your shirt, which I suppose I shall have to mend. For goodness' sake catch that pony and don't stand there looking so irritatingly calm.'

'Well, I can't see that there's anything to get worked up about,' answered David sulkily. 'Christo Carstairs says that all the best riders begin by falling off, and I heard Noel Kettering tell Fanny Marlowe that not falling off doesn't prove you're a good rider; it may easily be a sign that you're very cautious or have a quiet pony.'

'And who is Noel Kettering?' asked Mrs Rice-Greene.

'Oh, a friend of Henry T's,' answered David. 'She jumped off three times with Eric Lawson before they agreed to tie. She's got a grey pony she won as a prize, and she's schooled it herself. She's a pretty good rider, I can tell you.'

The Marlowes' schooling was not very successful. Their jumps, consisting of bales of straw and pairs of hen-coops with planks across them, were erected in a small bumpy field next to the farmyard. Three Jersey calves watched Golly with large mild eyes, and the ducks would pause, on their way to the pond, to see what was going on. Fanny had first turn; she spent half of it refusing a bale of straw twenty times and the other half trying to teach Golly to rein-back, but, as she didn't know that you were supposed to use your legs, she didn't succeed very well and, after a great deal of tugging, she only managed to make Golly take one very small reluctant step.

Graham wanted to canter a figure-of-eight, but, as Golly disapproved of cantering in any direction except homewards and he couldn't manage her, they spent most of his turn swerving back to the gate. Then Deb mounted. She trotted down to the bottom of the field and came galloping back, Golly covering the ground as fast as she could and Deb's legs working like a windmill in a gale. They stopped dead at the gate.

'Oh, that was *super*,' shrieked Deb, sitting in an inelegant position on Golly's neck and rubbing her eyes which had come in violent contact with the bristly mane. 'That's the fastest I've ever been. Now I'm going to jump.'

Golly did her best to be obliging; she cleared all three hen-coop jumps beautifully.

'Higher, higher,' shrieked Deb triumphantly. 'I've jumped a clear round,' she boasted, bouncing about in the saddle.

'They don't go any higher, you know they don't,' said Graham.

'Yes, they do; with bricks,' said Deb, leaping off and leaving Golly loose as she rushed to fetch bricks from a stack by the barn. In a few moments the hen-coop jumps were all about three inches higher, but, just as Deb was going to ride at them, Hubert – the gander – appeared escorting two of his wives, Humble and Haggis. They began to inspect the course.

'Oh, shoo him away,' shrieked Deb. 'Go on, Graham.'

Graham was not at all keen for Hubert was particularly fierce at that moment, because Haggis had two goslings – Hinder and Handicap – and Hint, his third wife, was sitting on eight eggs by the straw rick.

'Shoo him yourself,' said Graham.

'Oh, all right,' answered Deb; 'but you are a hopeless drip. Fancy being afraid of a measly old gander.'

'I'm not afraid,' answered Graham; 'but I've only got shorts on, and it jolly well hurts if he pecks your legs.'

All three children chivvied Hubert for a few moments and at

last, squawking indignantly, he led his wives away. Deb and Golly jumped another clear round.

'Hurray, hurray!' shrieked Deb, patting Golly's fat black neck frantically. 'I always knew that you could jump. Quick, some more bricks; I want to try higher.'

Fanny and Graham, nearly as excited as Deb by this sudden improvement in Golly's jumping, rushed for more bricks. Once again Golly cleared the jumps. This time they all patted her.

'There, your turn's over now, Deb,' said Fanny. 'Let's take her into the kitchen and give her something before we turn her out.'

'Oh, but I must have one more jump,' said Deb; 'just one.' They argued for a little, and then Fanny gave in.

'All right,' she said; 'but only one, mind, and it's an extra, because your turn's over.'

They raised one of the jumps, but this time, instead of flying over, Golly refused.

'Oh, I knew that would happen,' wailed Fanny.

'Use your legs,' said Graham, trying to imitate Henry Thornton's voice.

'You horrid lazy pony,' scolded Deb. Then she patted Golly, and said, 'Now, come on, try.'

But Golly had had enough; she knew what Deb was like; she refused to do anything but canter to the gate. It took ages to persuade her to jump and then it was only over a bar on two bricks, which was so small that it hardly counted as a jump.

'It was all your fault, Deb,' said Fanny as they hurried in to lunch. 'Now, poor Golly hasn't had any reward for being good, and next time she'll probably be as bad as ever.'

'Who's going to ride her on Monday? That's what I want to know,' said Graham. 'We can't keep changing; Colonel What's-his-name won't like it. I think we'd better draw lots.'

The Barbersleys never schooled their ponies, but on Saturday they decided to go for a ride. Swift and Swansdown had rested the day before and they were feeling rather fresh, which didn't please Helen and Jannice at all. They were no sooner outside the gate than Swift shied at a piece of paper, and jumping round, cannoned into Swansdown.

'Get out of the way, for goodness' sake,' screamed Helen in a voice that was both cross and frightened.

'Oh,' said Jannice, taking a firm hold of the mane. 'Oh, do stop, Helen; you're knocking me over.'

'Don't be such a silly little fool,' said Helen, when she had managed to wrench Swift round again. 'Why did you have to get in the way?'

'I didn't,' said Jannice tearfully.

'You did,' contradicted Helen. 'You're always doing something silly.'

'You're a liar, and I hate you,' said Jannice.

Helen gave a scornful sniff. 'Fat lot I care,' she said.

Then they met a bus and, though their ponies were perfectly quiet in traffic, they both began to shorten their reins.

'Whoa, whoa,' said Helen, clutching at Swift's mouth. 'Keep off my heels, Jannice.'

'Oh, stop the bus; oh, do stop it,' wailed Jannice, who was holding the mane too firmly to raise a hand. 'I know Swansdown is going to bolt.'

The ponies jogged a little, but that was all. Soon they turned up a sandy track, which led to some rather dreary-looking fields, fenced with wire and over-grazed by cattle waiting to be sold at the market.

'Oh, don't let's canter,' wailed Jannice. 'Please, Helen, don't let's canter.'

But Helen, hanging on to Swift's mouth and saying, 'Steady, boy, steady,' in a voice that was far from soothing, was not able to choose the pace. The ponies, feeling full of life, took charge and set off at a gallop across the fields. They didn't buck or shy, and neither Helen nor Jannice was unseated, but Jannice was firmly convinced that she had been bolted with, and Helen said that Swift was an unstoppable brute.

On the way home the ponies were less lively, Helen and Jannice stopped quarrelling and rode along together discussing the riding club. They agreed that the rally had been awful; that Henry Thornton was more stuck up than ever; that Noel Kettering thought she was the only person who could jump, and that it was cheek of people like them, Eric and Christo, to think that they could teach other people how to ride.

'Well, Colonel Sanderson will be there on Monday,' said Helen. 'Surely he'll stop them showing off.'

'I don't want to go,' said Jannice. 'I'll be made to jump. I'd

rather stay at home; I don't want to be a member at all.'
'But you've paid your subscription,' objected Helen.

Christo Carstairs, schooling in the big field at the end of Radney
Avenue, wished that her brothers had something better to do
than sit on the gate and make silly remarks. She knew that they
were only trying to be funny, but she found it very distracting
when they shouted, 'Can't that old nag go any faster?' in the
middle of her extended trotting, or, 'What about a gallop?' when
she was trying to rein-back. 'We can run faster than that,' they
yelled when she cantered. 'Oh, well hit, sir,' they cried, clapping
loudly when Dragonfly knocked down the jumps. At last she
had a brainwave.

'I say,' she said, riding across to them, 'remember that we're
going to the Forders' party this afternoon. I've got a feeling that
your tennis shorts are still waiting to be washed. Do you think
you'd better go and ask Mummy?'

The thought of appearing at the Forders' party in jeans was
too much for the boys; they dashed down the road. Christo sighed
with relief. She tried jumping again, but it was hopeless. She
could not prevent Dragonfly from rushing her fences and, if she
did not actually knock them down, she would only clear them
by a hairsbreadth.

It was no good going on like this, thought Christo. She would
have to take either Noel's or Eric's advice. But whose should she
take? She would wait until Monday, she decided; perhaps Colonel Sanderson would solve her problem.

Paulina Swindon didn't ride on Saturday because she was going
to the Forders' party. At her mother's suggestion she took it easy
all morning. She put on her dark glasses and carried a deck-chair
to the paved part of the garden. Sitting between the lily pond and
the rockery, she looked at *Riding*, mended her tennis socks and
then listened idly to the hum of the heavily-laden bees, watched
the antics of the goldfish and tried to develop an even and becoming suntan.

Juliet Naughton had invited Alex to ride over on Saturday
afternoon and jump her jumps. It was very good-natured of her,
because she was afraid that Oscar would kick Romeo or Toma-

hawk and she was certain that he would break the jumps. Alex, riding the short distance which lay between The Poplars and Greengates – the Naughtons' house – wondered why on earth he had accepted. To please Aunt Esmé and because Juliet had been so insistent, he supposed, but at least it was better than walking round the golf course watching his aunt and uncle play. Not that he would have minded going with them if they would have let him pursue his thoughts in peace, but they talked brightly and explained the uses of clubs and shots, determined that he should not feel left out. Juliet was waiting at the green gate.

'Hallo,' she said. 'We're all ready. Roly's holding the ponies.' And she led the way to the field, which lay behind the square house of faded red brick and joined the Vicarage Farm land.

'What marvellous jumps!' exclaimed Alex.

Of course Oscar did break one of the Naughtons' poles and Alex refused to jump anything else, until Juliet insisted that he should try Romeo. Alex found him very easy and comfortable to ride after Oscar. He jumped all the fences, with only one run out, and then he had a gallop round the field.

'Gosh!' said Alex as, rather red in the face, he pulled Romeo up beside Juliet. 'Gosh, he can go! That was much the fastest I've ever been.' He jumped off and patted him.

'I'm glad you like him,' said Juliet, smiling. She was delighted to have Romeo praised.

'Now try Tomahawk.' invited Roly. 'He can shift, I'll tell you. Come on; you may as well.'

'He feels very peculiar after Romeo; lovely, but in quite a different way. I suppose neither of you would like to try Oscar?' asked Alex as he picked up his reins.

'Well, I was going to suggest that we had a stone-and-box race,' answered Juliet, 'so we really want Roly to hold the stones. Do you think Oscar would stand tied to the gate?'

'Oh, yes,' answered Alex; 'one of his few accomplishments is tying up.'

The afternoon was followed by a wonderful tea. Mrs Naughton was one of those mothers who enjoy making cakes and who spend hours icing them, and yet don't seem to mind at all when their families devour hours of labour in two minutes. Juliet and Roly both talked at once and Mr and Mrs Naughton put a word in edgeways whenever they had the opportunity. Alex found it both restful and merry; he was sorry when the time came for him to go.

'Good-bye,' he said, riding away on Oscar. 'Thank you very much indeed for having me; I've enjoyed myself.'

On Saturday morning Noel and Henry schooled Sonnet and Echo for three-quarters of an hour, then Noel changed to Trappist and they took him and Echo out for a short ride. The schooling was successful except that Echo still didn't seem completely confident of his bit at the trot, and he bucked and went behind it at the canter.

'Of course I don't think he's really ready to canter round a school yet,' Noel had told Henry. And Henry, though he had replied that she was a fusspot and even more particular than his Uncle George, had taken her advice and used the whole field for his work at the canter and kept Echo cantering at a faster pace.

Noel enjoyed riding Trappist and Echo behaved more sensibly than usual. Henry began to talk of entering him for shows. 'Finch says he'll win a middle-weight hunter class,' he told Noel, 'that is if he behaves himself, which seems almost an impossibility.'

They were lingering in the stable-yard, leaning on doors and talking to Finch after their ride, when Henry suddenly remembered that they were supposed to be spending the afternoon at the Forders' tennis party.

'Oh, lord,' he said. 'I completely forgot the beastly function. *Can* you play tennis, Noel? You can borrow a racket. Oh, whatever made me accept? I don't feel the least like playing. I think I'll ring up and say we're ill.'

'I've only played at school,' said Noel rather dubiously. 'I'm not at all good. What are the Forders like, very superior?'

'No, they're quite possible,' answered Henry; 'but all the same, I think we'll be ill.'

Mrs Thornton refused to hear of Henry's pretending to be ill. She said that it was his duty to take part in social events; that he wasn't to neglect his tennis and that Noel couldn't possibly want to spend another afternoon wandering round the place doing nothing.

Chapter 5

THE day of Colonel Sanderson's rally was grey and overcast. The rain, which had fallen heavily all night, had spoiled the appearance of the jumps, carefully white-washed by Noel and Henry the afternoon before, and made the ground slippery and soggy.

Christo was the first person to arrive. She had started very early, for she felt that it would be a frightful sign of inefficiency if the secretary were to be late, and the Radney Riding Club might be blacklisted for ever by Colonel Sanderson. She looked round the field and thought that it looked very smart. Henry and Noel had done a good job. The Marlowes arrived next, Graham, who had drawn the longest lot, on Golly and the others on bicycles. Then the Naughtons and Paulina rode up together, followed by Alex, and after him came David, rather nervous lest he was late.

At twenty minutes past two, just as Henry was beginning to moan about Eric's unpunctuality and Noel was wondering whether this was the right day, the Lawsons' car and trailer arrived with Eric, his parents, Princess and Colonel Sanderson on board.

Juliet said, 'The Barbersleys still aren't here.'

'Oh, they'll turn up in a minute, I expect,' answered Christo.

'Curse these people who are always late,' muttered Henry, and he rode forward to be introduced to Colonel Sanderson.

However, Eric, not being versed in social etiquette, left the Colonel to talk to his parents, unboxed Princess, mounted and joined the other members in the field. The Colonel and the Lawson parents continued to stand by the car; they were discussing a horsy character called Toddy Hislop, and whether his hunter should have won at the Carlton Show.

At last, Henry, unable to bear waiting any longer, rode up to the Colonel, and said, 'We've marked out a school for you in the field here, sir.'

'Too small, much too small,' said the Colonel, when he saw the school. 'It's not big enough to keep canaries in, much less this crowd of animals. Ride round in a large circle – larger than that. Outside all the jumps.'

He sat on his shooting-stick in the middle of the circle, and Eric's parents joined him. They began to discuss whether Jim Stacey's Flower of May would have been in the money at the Clareshire Show, much less beaten the renowned Undaunted Star, if Brownie Sutcliffe, one of the judges, hadn't sold her to the Staceys.

'I'm told they paid the very dickens of a price,' said Mr Lawson.

'Still, I think Brownie's straight; straighter than most, anyway,' said the Colonel.

The members of the Radney Riding Club rode round and round and round. Henry was fuming and cursing beneath his breath. Alex was inventing a rally at which Oscar behaved marvellously and jumped four feet. David was watching a butterfly, Paulina was humming. Noel was wondering if the Colonel's mind had become a blank, as hers did in emergencies, and he couldn't remember how to begin a rally. But tall and solidly built, with a large nose and a clipped moustache, dressed in a brown tweed suit and a Homburg hat, with the brim turned down, the Colonel didn't look like the sort of person whose mind became a blank. He looked organizing, military and obstinate, decided Noel. Christo was thinking, well, I suppose he'll begin sometime, but I wish he'd buck up, when Roly turned in his saddle and shouted to Graham:

'Isn't he ever going to stop gassing?'

'Roly,' said Juliet in shocked tones.

'Well, I'm tired of walking round and Tomahawk's getting giddy,' answered her brother.

At last the Colonel gave the order to trot. Eric, in the lead, trotted on rather fast. He sat in the back of his saddle with his reins rather long and he was inclined to look down. Christo, who was behind him, was having trouble with Dragonfly. But she didn't become fussed; she thought, oh, well, if he sees her misbehaving perhaps he'll give me some good advice.

Henry couldn't make Echo trot properly. He refused to go at a steady pace, and every now and then he bucked or leaped in the air. Sonnet was going well; but Noel, having an attack of the needle, was looking down and her legs felt like chewed string. Paulina, still humming, was riding on Sonnet's tail; Juliet, David, Roly and Graham were in a bunch. Miles behind everyone rode Alex, kicking frantically to keep Oscar trotting.

Colonel Sanderson told them to canter. Eric cantered on slowly, but Princess's nose was in the air, she was fussing with her bit and not going quite straight. Echo gave three bucks and cantered on the wrong leg. Dragonfly couldn't canter as slowly as Princess; she fly-jumped and fought her bit until Christo passed Eric and took the lead.

Paulina was sitting in the back of her saddle giving an occasional kick, blissfully unaware that Starshine was on the wrong leg. Juliet was hanging down over Romeo's shoulder trying to tell which leg she was on. Tanzy, with her mouth open and her head in the air was galloping all over the field followed by Tomahawk; Roly resting his hands on the fat roan neck, merely made a noise that was supposed to sound like an express train, and Golly and Oscar were still trotting. Colonel Sanderson seemed to have lost interest. Noel decided that he had been struck dumb by the low standard of riding.

'Halt,' shouted the Colonel at last, when nearly everyone was galloping and Tanzy had narrowly missed being kicked by Oscar. 'Ride assemble in the centre of the manège.'

'What's that?' asked Roly loudly, when he had stopped Tomahawk by riding him into Romeo. 'It sounds like a zoo.' And he began to growl ferociously.

'What sort of noise do elephants make?' he asked Graham.

'They trumpet, of course,' yelled Graham in reply.

'Can't you kids keep quiet?' said Eric disagreeably as he lined up.

'Kids are baby goats,' said Roly. 'Maa-aa, that's the sort of noise they make. I was being a bear.'

'Roly,' said Juliet.

'Shush,' said Christo.

'Now,' said Colonel Sanderson, clearing his throat. 'I'm going to show you a good seat.' He beckoned to Paulina. A low whistle escaped from Eric. Smiling brightly, Paulina rode out in front of the ride.

'Now here we have a good seat,' said the Colonel. 'She sits well down in her saddle, straight back, long reins, legs well forward, heels and hands low. There's not much to correct there. Now, I want to see you all sitting like that,' he went on. 'Well down in your saddles, not perched on the pommel like a lot of Italian monkeys.'

Eric laughed politely. Henry scowled and Noel wondered what

would happen if Colonel Sanderson ever set foot in West Barset-shire.

'A good all-round utility seat,' he was saying, 'that's what we want; utility, not a lot of fancy theories.'

Paulina was trying not to look too pleased. But, really, out in front of *everyone*. Eric and Henry and everyone. It was too shattering, she heard herself telling her parents.

'Lead on, left rein,' said the Colonel to Eric. 'Now sit down, sit back, legs forward.'

Henry rode beside Noel for a moment.

'The man's mad,' he muttered. 'I could wring his neck and Eric's and that silly Paulina's.'

When Colonel Sanderson had everyone sitting somewhere near the cantle, he decided that they should do some drill. With a great deal of numbering to the left they were divided into two sec-tions and the Colonel tried to drill them. Unfortunately, his com-mands were rather involved, and no one seemed to understand them except, perhaps, Eric and Christo. Noel kept forgetting her number and which way was right and which left; she was al-ways bad at this sort of thing. Graham couldn't make Golly keep up, and David couldn't control Tanzy at all. He kept galloping past the people ahead of him or charging about the field when he was meant to be circling. Oscar kicked at everyone who came near him, and Alex, red in the face and kicking frantically, was quite unable to make him keep in a pair with Juliet. Just as the Col-onel was begnning to lose his temper the Barbersleys rode into the field.

'What's this?' demanded Colonel Sanderson, as they tried to join in the drill. 'Late on parade?'

'It looks like it, sir,' said Eric, when the Barbersleys had failed to answer.

'Well, the least they can do is to apologize,' stormed the Colonel. 'It's disgraceful. Can't you teach your members some manners? Late and not a word, not a word of apology.' His puffy face be-came purple and all the members felt very embarrassed.

'Say you're sorry, you idiots,' hissed Christo.

'Go and apologize,' muttered Henry, wishing that the idea of running a riding club had never entered his head.

Helen looked mulish.

Jannice whispered, 'Oh, I can't. You say it, Helen.'

There was a pause and then Helen said, 'I couldn't help it. Swansdown lost a shoe. We started late, and Jannice couldn't make her hurry. I'm sick and tired of trying to get them along.'.

'I couldn't help it,' said Jannice to Noel. 'All my old nervousness came back. Swansdown was trying to bolt and Helen would go so fast.'

Colonel Sanderson gave Helen a sharp lecture on the rank carelessness of not checking your pony's shoes, and asked her what she thought would have happened in wars if the cavalry had been so careless. Helen, looking extremely sulky, refused to answer. Then the Colonel announced that they would do some jumping. Most people sighed with relief, but when he told everyone to cross their stirrups and knot their reins, relief turned to apprehension except for Noel and Eric. The Colonel had the bar on petrol drums, the hurdles and the brush fence arranged at right angles to the hedge, and the poles from the triple were used as wings for the hedgeless side.

'Come along, come along,' shouted the Colonel at the nervous people, who were wondering if the order to cross stirrups really included them.

Jannice had gone green with terror, but she didn't dare argue. Eric jumped first. It was child's play to him and Princess. Eric folded his arms and sent her on with his legs at each fence just as the Colonel directed, but, for Christo, who followed, it was not so easy. Dragonfly seized the opportunity to jump at a full-speed gallop; she crashed through the hurdles and almost fell at the brush. Echo, excited by the two horses which had jumped ahead of him, jumped very fast, taking off too far away, and after the last fence he gave three terrific bucks; Henry was almost off, but he grabbed the reins and pulled Echo's head up.

'Ha, ha,' laughed Colonel Sanderson. 'That'll teach you to sit back, my boy.'

Noel and Sonnet were quite at home; they had often done this sort of thing before, but Paulina was nervous and let Starshine run out despite the wings. At her next attempt the Colonel waved his shooting-stick and Starshine jumped. Juliet, who fell off over the third fence, didn't make any fuss, but Helen who came off at the first, said that she had hurt her arm and couldn't she sit down for a little?

The Colonel gave them both a short lecture about keeping

their legs farther forward, and then called David out to jump. Tanzy didn't like the idea at all; she charged about the field with her mouth open and David, leaning well back, with his legs well forward, was quite unable to present her at the first jump, much less drop his reins and fold his arms.

At last, Colonel Sanderson managed to catch Tanzy; he led her up to the first fence and saying, 'Sit tight,' he let her go and hit her over the quarters with his shooting-stick.

She leaped forward and then cat-jumped. David hung on by the reins, jagging her in the mouth. and then fell off as she swerved away from the second fence and galloped off across the field. While Henry, Noel, Eric, Christo and David were catching Tanzy, Roly fell off Tomahawk three times and both he and Graham were finally given up as hopeless without having jumped the brush. Oscar paid so little attention to Colonel Sanderson's stick-waving that Mr Lawson was sent to the car to fetch a hunting-whip, and while he was away Tanzy was chased over another jump. David came off again, and Jannice, looking absolutely terrified, clutching her pommel and leaning back, was carried over all three fences by an intimidated Swansdown. Jannice didn't fall off, but she seemed on the verge of tears. Then it was Oscar's turn again and this time the Lawson parents helped the Colonel.

'Shoo, shoo; chase him over,' shouted Mrs Lawson flapping a mackintosh.

'Get on, you brute. Grrh,' roared Colonel Sanderson, waving his arms and shooting-stick like a madman. Mr Lawson cracked and waved the whip. But all in vain. Oscar, quite unperturbed, trotted up to the jump and refused again and again.

At last, Mr Lawson, tired of whip-cracking, hit Oscar across his quarters. Oscar replied with a kick which caught Mr Lawson on the thigh and sent him flying. Henry and Noel, who had been watching the noisy scene with heavy hearts, exchanged glad glances and only just controlled their smiles. Eric rode forward in consternation; Mrs Lawson ran to her husband's aid. Alex was apologizing. Mr Lawson said several words which Eric only used at school, sat up and finally climbed gingerly to his feet.

'It's all right,' he said at last; 'nothing broken.'

'Well, you haven't the pony to thank for that,' said Mrs Lawson indignantly. 'He meant it, the little brute, if ever I saw one that did.'

'Yes, by jove. He ought to be cast for vice,' agreed Colonel Sanderson.

'He's certainly not what I'd call a child's pony,' said Mr Lawson, with a forced laugh.

'No, no; not at all,' said the Colonel and, turning to Alex, he added, 'This pony of yours — he's a dangerous brute. You tell your parents that they ought to pass him on. Yes, that's it; pass him on before he does any *real* damage.'

'Yes, sir,' answered Alex, his face expressionless.

'Well, now then,' said Colonel Sanderson, looking round him, 'where had we got to?'

All the members — even Eric — had been hoping that the rally was over; now their hope and their faces fell. Most of them looked beseechingly at Henry. Surely he could do something. I don't believe he'll ever stop, thought Noel. Christo thought, it doesn't get dark till about nine.

'I think, sir,' said Henry after a moment's hesitation, 'that, as it is already half-past four, we can hardly trespass on your kindness by asking you to stay any longer. We fully appreciate the time and trouble you have taken to come here today, and I should like to thank you very much indeed on behalf of all our members.'

'Hear, hear,' said Eric. Christo began to clap, everyone joined in quite cheerfully now that they knew that the rally was over.

Roly and Graham chanted, 'Hear, hear,' in various strange and unnatural voices.

'Delighted to have been of any help,' said the Colonel. 'Remember what you have learned today, practise it and one fine morning you will wake up to find yourselves horsemen. Don't you believe these fellas who want to keep you in a riding-school for the best years of your lives. All a horseman needs is a good nerve, plenty of experience and a few tips like the ones I've given you this afternoon.'

'Good night and thank you very much,' said Henry, for the rally seemed to be over.

'Good night,' echoed the other members, and most of them rode away down the drive; some dejectedly alone, others in chattering groups. As Henry rode to the stable-yard he increased his despair by imagining what they were all saying. Eric began to box Princess. Christo followed Henry and Noel round to the stables.

Henry dismounted with a groan.

'Lord, what a day,' he said, sitting down on the mounting-block and putting his head in his hands. 'What an appalling day. I shall never hold up my head in Radney again.'

'But seriously, Henry, what did you think of him?' asked Christo.

'Think of him,' exploded Henry. 'That's just the point; I daren't let myself think of him; I shall blow up with rage if I do. It's my own fault, I know. I ought to have realized that Eric was certain to produce some miserable diehard. Anyway, the riding club is just about wrecked. You'd better send everyone back their subscriptions; it's more dignified than waiting until they demand them.'

'Oh, rot,' said Christo. And Noel, who had been unsaddling Sonnet and had arrived in time to hear Henry's last remark, said:

'Don't be such a defeatist, Henry. Besides, we'll have to hold one more rally to undo the evil of this day.'

'Yes, we'd better have it quite soon,' said Christo, 'and get someone sensible to instruct.'

'And how are we to tell if they're sensible?' demanded Henry. 'If by sensible you mean enlightened. We need someone who's studied equitation, not a bucolic hunting type.'

'I hope the dear Colonel's gone,' said Noel. 'You're yelling rather. Do you think I'd better go and see?'

'I don't care if he does hear,' said Henry. 'I'm fed up with everyone. It's obviously impossible to learn to ride properly in this miserable country.' He led Echo into his box, banged the door shut and began to unsaddle him.

'I'd better go,' said Christo to Noel. 'It's a pity everything was such a flop. Do you think Henry really means to give the whole thing up?' she asked as she mounted.

'Heaven knows,' said Noel wearily. 'But after tea he may feel better.'

'Yes, that's what I thought,' said Christo. 'I'll ring up tomorrow morning and see which way the land lies.'

Noel watched Dragonfly's black quarters disappear down the drive and then she wandered slowly to the forage-room to fetch Echo and Sonnet their feeds.

Chapter 6

NOEL and Henry found themselves quite unable to think about the riding club in a cool, calm or collected manner for the rest of Monday evening. Every time it was mentioned they found themselves fuming with rage at the iniquities of Colonel Sanderson and the Lawson family. To make matters worse, Mr and Mrs Thornton were out to dinner and bridge with some elderly neighbours. Left alone, Henry and Noel found it impossible to prevent the conversation reverting to the dismal topic. In despair they each took a detective story and read as they ate their dinner and until they went to bed.

On Tuesday morning, having worked off the remains of their fury by describing the rally to Finch, they schooled for an hour and then took the horses out for a ride. In between Echo's bouts of bucking they discussed the future of the riding club.

'Of course,' said Henry, 'even if Sanderson had been any good he would have found it almost impossible to teach us anything. We're all at such hopelessly different stages. If only the Marlowes, David, Roly, Alex and those maddening Barbersleys could either get on a bit or be taught separately it wouldn't be so difficult. At least the rest of us can stop and start and steer after a fashion.'

'I think that we ought to try to find someone to instruct the bad people quickly,' said Noel, feeling relieved that Henry had decided to carry on with the club. 'Honestly, they're so bad that they'd be a disgrace to any pony club.'

'It's true,' said Henry. 'I think we'd better ring up Christo when we get home,' he went on, after a short silence, 'and I thought we might write to Uncle George and ask him if any enlightened equitation experts live round here. He's only in France at present, so we should soon get a reply.'

Christo was very helpful over the telephone. She said that she was sure that she could think of several people to instruct and she would rack her brains and bicycle over to Radney that afternoon to discuss the club programme. When she arrived, directly after lunch, Henry and Noel took her into the morning-room, which, being at the back of the house, looked out to the east and was supposed to catch the early morning sun and to possess a magnificent view. Unfortunately, owing to the unexpected growth of some supposedly dwarf shrubs it was dark and damp and had no view at all. It was a miserable room in winter, according to Henry, but cool on the hottest summer day and its best point was that no grown-up ever entered it, so they would not be disturbed.

'We oughtn't really to meet without Eric,' said Henry. 'At least, I'm sure that it must be against all committee rules and regulations, but, if I see him before Monday's mournful memories have faded a little, I might go berserk.'

Christo had thought of four possible people to instruct what Henry called the Hopeless, and she referred to more politely as the second string. The first person was Joan Summer, who had won the Grade C jumping at the Waylebury show.

'She's about twenty,' said Christo, 'and she's got three horses – two show-jumpers and a youngster which she's breaking in – and Mummy says that she believes she's got a teaching diploma of some sort.'

'But candidly,' said Henry, trying not to sound squashing, 'I don't think she'll do. She does jump, I know, and she may have a diploma, but consider her leg position.'

'Well, then, there's Mr Gunstone. He hunts,' said Christo; 'but I can't say I've studied his leg position.'

Henry screwed up his nose. 'Gunstone's the local vet,' he explained to Noel. 'He's not a bad vet, but he's never struck me as being much of a horseman.'

'What about Mrs Helspeth then?' asked Christo. 'She used to run a riding-school before she married.'

'She's a bit of a hag,' said Henry. 'She wears grey flowing cloaks and her husband's hats,' he told Noel. 'And she's always being taken up for half-starving that herd of ponies. Besides, everyone says she's certifiable.'

'Some people say that she's terribly brainy and a marvellous teacher,' countered Christo.

'Well, I don't think she's the person for us,' said Henry. 'She'll give Deb and Roly nervous breakdowns; they'll think she's a witch.'

'When you're that age you like witches,' argued Christo.

'Anyway, the only other person I've thought of is your sister Elizabeth, and I don't suppose you'll think she's any good.'

'No, I don't. Frankly, I think she'd finish the club off,' said Henry. 'For one thing she doesn't agree with our principles; she thinks you're mad if you school your horse and she can't bear the mention of dressage.'

'Well, I just don't know what to do for you,' said Christo in rather disgruntled tones. 'I don't see how the second string are to be taught. It's hopeless expecting to get a first-class instructor for such awful material. You just can't; you'll have to put up with second best.'

Henry sighed. 'You must admit,' he said, 'that it's worse than useless to have them taught by the Sandersons of the world.'

'But it's true that you can't ask equitation experts to teach beginners,' said Noel, 'and that's what the second string count as. Personally, I think you and Christo will have to teach them yourselves. You haven't had my teaching experience, but at least you know the correct leg position, which is more than most people round here seem to.'

'But I don't know the correct leg position,' objected Christo. 'At least I'm not at all sure that I do.'

'And I've no patience,' said Henry. 'I can talk and spew forth theories, but as for teaching – '

'You'll have to abandon the second string then,' said Noel rather crossly.

'You could teach them, Noel,' said Henry in the voice of one who makes a discovery. 'You'd be rather good. You know far more than you pretend, or, anyway, you ought after such constant association with my esteemed Uncle George.'

'But I'm only here for these holidays,' Noel pointed out. 'I can't be on the permanent staff. Besides, I always forget everything if I have the needle, and you know I'll have it if I have to instruct anyone – much less a whole ride. And I'm too young; Alex isn't much younger than me, you know, and Helen Barbersley's older; they'd be terribly offended if they were taught by a person of their own age.'

'Objections overruled,' said Henry. 'If you're bullying Christo and me into teaching, you can jolly well help.'

'Hear, hear,' said Christo.

'And any of the second string who are too superior to be taught by us can resign,' added Henry.

They decided that, if enough of the second string were able to come, they would hold a rally on the following day. Then they wrote a letter to Major Holbrooke, asking him to suggest a suitable expert to instruct the senior members of the club. They described the Sanderson rally, and ended with a great many polite wishes for the health and enjoyment of both the Major and Mrs Holbrooke.

'There,' said Henry, 'written out again in my best handwriting and punctuated by my highest standard of punctuation, it ought to please any uncle. Would you two like to go and ring up the second string?'

Everyone, except the Barbersleys, said that they could come, and Juliet, who was supposed to count as a senior, asked if she could come as well as Roly, as she was sure that she didn't know half as much as Henry, Noel and Christo.

Then Henry drew a picture of the correct leg position for Christo, who was beginning to panic about the rally, and Noel wrote out the correct aids for the rein-back and the turn on the forehand. Saying that she would study their diagrams and instructions far into the night, and that she would send Major Holbrooke's letter from Trawley post office, Christo mounted her bicycle, which – to Noel's indignation – had no name, and pedalled briskly away, despite the heat of the afternoon.

At ten o'clock next morning Christo re-appeared on Dragonfly, who was wearing a snaffle and a very new-looking drop noseband.

'If you don't mind,' she said, 'I'm coming to school with you. I'm fed up with trying to reform this mad animal on my own. I can't stop her at all in this outfit you recommended, Noel, and she never seems to improve.'

Henry said that it was a pleasure to have Christo. Finch said that Dragonfly was a nice-looking little mare, and Noel pointed out that drop nosebands weren't magical; it was schooling that improved the horse; and then they rode out to the field. They exercised their mounts round the field for a short time, and then Noel began to school seriously, but she was soon interrupted by Henry.

'Come and take us,' he said. 'You've no idea how dreadfully smug you look basking in the light of knowledge while Christo and I wander with a wailing and a gnashing of teeth through the darkness of utter ignorance. Come on, you must know what's wrong with our horses.'

'Yes, be a sport,' said Christo.

'Stand there,' said Henry. 'We'll ride round.'

'But I don't know what's wrong,' wailed Noel. 'If I did, I'd tell you what to do. I can see that they don't go properly, that they've no tempo or anything, but I've no idea what to do about it.'

'Just tell us exactly what *is* wrong,' said Christo, and they began to ride round at a walk.

'Well?' asked Henry when Noel had watched them in silence for several moments. 'Come on, let's have it; we're not perfect, are we?'

'N-no,' said Noel. 'Echo isn't walking out; he ought to look purposeful as though he were trying to get somewhere, but he wanders and dawdles.'

'I'm using my legs till they're almost dropping off,' said Henry.

'Dragonfly takes short quick steps,' said Noel. 'She ought to take longer and slower ones. Can you give her a looser rein, Christo? If you ride her on a very long rein she might stretch her neck out, and then begin to take a longer stride.'

'She'll jog,' said Christo, 'or go off at a gallop or something. You don't know what a mad animal she is.'

'If she jogs pull her up to a walk and then give her a loose rein quickly,' said Noel. 'That's better.'

'Here, I want some attention, teacher,' grumbled Henry. 'I don't see why Christo should have it all. Am *I* walking any better?'

'No,' answered Noel frankly. 'Your legs are beginning to look like Deb Marlowe's and they're not having much effect.'

'If you knew what they felt like,' grumbled Henry. 'Prepare to halt,' he shouted at Christo.

'Awful,' said Noel as they halted. 'Echo looks like a cab horse – he's resting a leg – and Christo, you stopped much too suddenly; I don't believe you used your legs.'

'Should you use your legs for halting?' asked Christo. Noel and Henry both gave groans of horror.

'Shut your fingers, as an indication that you are about to halt, close your legs, put your shoulders back and feel the reins until the horse begins to halt,' said Henry.

'We'll walk on and try again.'

They schooled for ages and neither of the horses improved much. At the trot, Dragonfly's quick short steps degenerated into a sort of hop which wasn't a pace at all. Echo's trot was rapid and tempoless, particularly round corners. Noel racked her brain for advice. If only the Major were here, she thought; once he had pointed out a fault one could see it, and when he suggested a cure it was not difficult to carry it out.

'I don't know,' she said hopelessly, pushing her long dark hair from her face. 'I'm not experienced enough. I just can't give you advice.'

'Supposing we try changing from an ordinary trot into an extended one,' said Henry. 'Echo needs waking up; he has no impulsion at all.'

'What about giving them some schooling at the canter?' suggested Christo, who was feeling bored.

'You could do some cantering round the field,' said Noel; 'but I can't see any point in cantering round the school when they can't even walk or trot; you'll only get them even more behind the bit than they are already.'

'But they can walk and trot,' said Christo, 'it's only that they don't do it perfectly.'

'By dressage standards, they can't even halt,' said Henry, with an angry laugh.

'But we can't judge ordinary horses by dressage standards,' objected Christo. 'I mean, dressage is only for tests. I don't mind Dragonfly being no good for tests; I'd rather jump anyway.'

Noel swallowed back some angry words and said, quite calmly, 'Dressage is schooling and, therefore, dressage standards are the only standards which *can* apply. Dressage tests are for the keen people to check up on their schooling, to see that it has been on the right lines and, as they grow more advanced, to see how perfectly you can train your horse to carry out a series of difficult movements.'

'You sound as though you're quoting Uncle George,' said Henry. 'But it's true, Christo, and until you school your horse properly – in other words, by dressage standards – you won't win your jumping classes.'

'I seem to have put my foot in it again,' said Christo. 'But I did warn you that I knew nothing. But look here,' she went on, after a pause, 'Eric doesn't know anything about dressage, does he? And yet he wins enough.'

'No, Eric doesn't know a thing about it,' said Henry. 'He calls it a stunt. But you wouldn't see him winning so much in West Barsetshire or anywhere else where the ponies are properly schooled. A jumper doesn't need to learn more than elementary dressage. He has to be supple and well balanced, and he has to come back to hand when you want him and to increase his pace when you tell him, and that's what elementary dressage teaches. You must admit that you'd like to be able to hold back Dragon-fly a little longer.'

'If you had Eric and a member of the Olympic team in the same ring you'd see the difference,' observed Noel.

'I'm sure that I'm going to make some frightful gaffe this afternoon,' said Christo in rather disheartened accents. 'You're awfully rash to let me instruct.'

'We're not going to give them a disquisition on dressage,' said Henry. 'Don't worry, it'll be one long cry of "legs back" after Monday.'

Christo stayed to lunch. They ate brawn and salad, stewed plums and custard. Henry said that the brawn tasted foul and left his on the side of his plate. Afterwards they lay on the lawn and argued about poetry, and whether one should be made to learn it at school, until the vanguard of the second string arrived in the shape of Deb Marlowe on a bicycle.

'I bet you can't guess what's happened,' said Deb, rushing up to Henry as soon as he entered the stable-yard. 'It's terribly exciting; but I bet you can't guess why Graham hasn't biked over too.'

'I guess he's broken his leg in three places and been removed to Waylebury Infirmary,' said Henry with what he hoped was an American accent.

Deb giggled. 'You are silly,' she said. 'It's nothing like that; I told you it was exciting.'

'Well, he's been left a fortune then,' suggested Henry, 'by a rich uncle.'

'We haven't got one,' shrieked Deb; 'I mean, not a rich one; ours is terribly poor – Daddy has to lend *him* money.'

Henry began to grin.

'You shouldn't yell things about your family life in public,' said Christo in severe tones.

'I knew he'd never guess,' said Deb, not attending to Christo. 'Listen, there's hoofs. Come quickly and you'll see.'

She rushed down the back drive to the field gate; the others followed more sedately. Graham on Golly and Fanny on a grey pony, were riding up the drive together.

'It's Swansdown, isn't it?' asked Christo.

'Yes, we've got her on a week's trial,' yelled Deb, skipping about the drive. 'Daddy's going to buy her, so we shall all have lots more turns now.'

'Oh, shush, Deb,' said Fanny.

'Well, it's true,' yelled Deb, even louder.

'Yes, but there's no need to make such a noise about it,' said Fanny.

'Oh, don't be so *fussy*,' said Deb.

'What's happening to Jannice?' asked Christo. 'Is she having a new pony?'

'Oh, *no*,' said Deb. 'Haven't you heard? The silly thing's giving up riding. That awful Colonel just about finished her. She says she'll never mount another pony as long as she lives.'

'Oh, do be quiet, Deb,' said Fanny, for seeing Henry, Noel and Christo exchange glances, and feeling a tension in the atmosphere, she decided that Deb had said something tactless again.

'Hallo, roll out the barrel,' shouted Graham to Roly, as the Naughtons, followed by Alex, rode up the drive.

Henry opened the gate into the field. Noel began to move the school posts to an unpoached piece of ground. As soon as David arrived Henry asked Juliet to lead round at a walk and the three instructors stood together in the middle of the school, looking and feeling very self-conscious.

They found teaching very difficult. At first none of them spoke, and then they all shouted commands at the same moment, throwing the class into even worse disorder than before. Everyone had so many faults that it was difficult to know which fault to correct first. Henry concentrated on the leg positions, which, he said, were the key to the seat. Christo corrected hands because, she said, it was hard luck on the ponies to have their mouths pulled about. Noel, saying firmly that it was useless to correct the legs and hands of people who were sitting on the wrong part of the saddle, taught each member of the second string to sit in the middle of the saddle, with a handsbreadth between them and the top of the cantle, and then to adjust their stirrups. Unfortunately, though the pupils' seats improved, their ponies behaved as badly as ever. Oscar kicked at everyone and refused to trot without the most tremendous displays of energy on Alex's part. Tanzy galloped round the field with her mouth open whenever she was asked to canter. Tomahawk was willing, but Roly had no control over him. Swansdown and Golly were well behaved, but Golly had long since become inured to the Marlowes' constant kicking and ignored all aids unless she felt like obeying them. Juliet could control Romeo, but she seemed unable to produce the smallest spark of impulsion, despite the insults of the instructors, who told her that her mount looked like a milk-float pony, a dead donkey and a cab horse.

'Supposing,' suggested Noel when she realized that her fellow-instructors were fast becoming exasperated, 'that we taught two people each and tried to improve their ponies at the same time. It's almost impossible to do that at the moment when Tanzy and Tomahawk want quietening down and the rest waking up.'

'And Oscar wants sending to the knacker,' said Henry.

'Hear, hear, hear,' said Christo.

'Keep away from the others, Alex,' shouted Henry for about the sixth time, but he was too late. Oscar whirled round and kicked out; his heels thudded against Tomahawk's fat roan quarters.

'Oh, curse him,' said Henry.

'Why can't he keep him away?' asked Christo. 'They just won't ride a length apart.'

'I don't think it's altogether Alex's fault,' said Noel, as they hurried towards Tomahawk. 'Oscar seems beyond all hope. Even Eric couldn't do much with him.'

'It was lucky,' said Henry, examining Tomahawk for cuts, 'that he got him on the quarters and not the stifle or hock. Trot him on, Roly, and we'll see if he's lame.'

Tomahawk wasn't lame, but the three instructors stood with worried expressions wondering what to do about Oscar.

'He'll break someone's leg before he's finished,' said Henry, 'and then there'll be hell to pay.'

'Dozens of angry mothers on the doorstep,' said Christo. 'It would finish the riding club.'

'We shall have to find something else for Alex to ride,' said Noel. 'Apart from kicking, he'll never learn a thing on Oscar.'

'Can't his parents buy him another pony?' asked Henry.

'He lives with an unhorsy uncle and aunt,' explained Noel. 'I don't know if he has any parents.'

'I believe there's a father in the Navy,' said Christo.

'That doesn't sound very hopeful,' said Henry. 'Sailors aren't much use with horses.'

'Can't he borrow?' asked Noel. 'I always had to in my youth.'

'But what?' demanded Henry.

'I can't think of any ponies that aren't used regularly,' said Christo. Noel had thought of a pony, but she was hoping that the owner would suggest it.

At last Henry said, almost unwillingly, 'Well, I suppose he'd better borrow Trappist for today.'

'Oh, first-class idea,' said Christo.

Noel said, 'He'd better ride him in a snaffle, hadn't he? He can borrow Sonnet's.'

Noel and Alex took Oscar to the stables and saddled Trappist, who was brought in each day to avoid the flies.

'I am very much afraid,' said Alex suddenly, 'that I am causing everyone a great deal of inconvenience. I think that really it would be much better if I unjoined the club.'

'It's all very difficult,' said Noel; 'but, honestly, I don't think that one should give up learning to ride merely to avoid giving trouble to other people. I never had a pony of my own until Sonnet,' she went on as she bridled Trappist. 'I used to borrow and I never had any control over them. There was one – Topsy – she used to gallop me out of the ring at every gymkhana, and I once let her go all over a very smart garden at a pony club rally.'

Alex was delighted with Trappist; he said that he walked as though on air and that his long grey neck and pricked ears looked wonderful as they rose up in front of one. But he came in for a lot of criticism from Henry, for he found it very difficult to press with his calves instead of kicking, and to keep his body and hands still. Tanzy was still a blot on the proceedings. David seemed to have no control over her at all. Each time she began to misbehave, his long legs would shoot forward, his pale face would turn red and, with his hands alternately in his stomach and on Tanzy's withers, he would be galloped across the field. At last Noel turned him off and began to school Tanzy. Henry and Christo, deciding that the other ponies had had enough, declared the rally over and told the members that they would be holding another within the next day or two. The Naughtons thanked their instructors very politely, but the Marlowes, much to Christo's indignation, merely rode away laughing and chattering to each other.

'Beastly bad-mannered lot,' she complained. 'The least they can do is to say thank you.'

Chapter 7

IT was on Thursday at teatime, several days before Henry and Noel expected it, that Major Holbrooke's reply to their letter arrived. He had cabled from Nice.

'Up with Uncle George,' said Henry, opening the cable; 'he works fast. *Le General de Veriac, at the Flint House, Great Fingest, Longworth*,' he read. '*Mention my name. Be very polite. Writing. Holbrooke.*'

'Whatever on earth is that supposed to mean?' inquired Mrs Thornton. 'Has George taken leave of his senses?'

'No, no, no. It's our enlightened expert,' said Henry, dancing round the teatable. 'He's a Frenchman, obviously, and we're to be very polite – that means he's absolutely top class. Oh, well done, Uncle G.'

'Perhaps he won't be able to come,' said Noel gloomily. 'He may easily have dozens of previous engagements or a chronic cold on the chest.'

'I feel that the fates are with us this time,' said Henry. 'Uncle G.'s arrangements rarely misfire. I'm going to ring up Christo in a minute,' he added, sitting down and beginning to eat cress sandwiches at full speed.

'This doesn't mean *another* rally, I hope,' said Mrs Thornton.

'Oh, our programme's most comprehensive,' explained Henry. 'It contains four rallies for the second string, two for the seniors and a gymkhana before the end of the holidays.'

'It's too much,' said Mrs Thornton crossly. 'You're turning the place into a bear garden.'

'Well, you always used to say that I was self-centred,' replied Henry, 'and now you don't like my good works. You're very difficult to please, Mother. Besides, look at Uncle George, he has the whole pony club to *stay*.'

'George has always been good-natured to the point of foolishness,' answered Mrs Thornton, 'and there's no need for you to follow in his footsteps.'

'I've finished,' said Henry, drinking his tea at one gulp. 'If no one minds, I'll go and do my telephoning.'

'I dont know what your father is going to say to the telephone bill,' grumbled Mrs Thornton. But Henry had gone. Noel listened to Mrs Thornton for the five minutes which politeness demanded, before following Henry downstairs. She found him sprawled sideways on the hall sofa, with his feet dangling over the back.

'Hallo,' said Henry. 'Everything is moving at a terrific speed. Christo's delighted about de Veriac; we've discussed dates. She's calling a gymkhana meeting for tomorrow afternoon – they're all determined to have this beastly gymkhana – and I said we'd have the second string at two for an hour's schooling. Now come on, you've got to help me write this polite letter to the General.'

The letter took hours; they argued over every word, particularly in the polite parts. As Henry said, it was difficult to draw the line between politeness and over-effusiveness.

Then Henry spent what remained of the evening learning suitable French phrases.

'It would be just like Uncle George to send us an expert who knew no English,' he said. 'That's the sort of dirty trick which amuses him.'

The second string's second lesson was not much of a success; to Henry's annoyance and Noel's chagrin, they seemed to have forgotten everything which they had been taught at their first. They rode on each other's tails, flapped their legs as badly as ever and no one, except Alex and Juliet, could remember the aids for the turn on the forehand.

Henry decided that they were all half-witted and that it was a waste of time to try to teach them. Noel wished miserably that she were a better instructor. The pupils, tired of schooling and disheartened by the unconcealed scorn in Henry's voice, became dull and stupid.

'Surely they've had enough schooling,' remonstrated Christo at last. 'The poor kids were schooled for an hour and a half last time and they've already had thirty-five minutes today. Can't we give them some races or jumping now?'

'OK,' said Henry, who was tired of teaching. 'You and Noel carry on; I've shouted myself hoarse and, apart from that, I want to write out an agenda for the meeting.'

Noel and Christo divided the ride in two, Christo organizing a scavenge hunt and Noel taking the jumping section.

Noel, having borrowed Graham's belt, with which she made a neck-strap for Roly, put her pupils over several low jumps. When they had jumped one height well she made the fences wider rather than higher, explaining that in this way the ponies would learn to jump greater heights without being overfaced.

Then she changed pupils with Christo. Juliet and Alex were jumping well, and when they had both jumped several fences, first with, and then without, stirrups, she arranged a low course for them. But Tanzy, who had not been at all improved by Colonel Sanderson's methods, became upset as soon as she saw the jumps and careered about quite out of control. When David had had about twenty tries at a one-foot jump and failed to get Tanzy over, Noel turned him off. She managed to jump at her first attempt, but it was not easy for her to keep Tanzy calm or straight.

Henry, who had finished his agenda and come to watch, now said, 'You know I believe that pony would go better in a vulcanite pelham and a standing martingale. It's going to take months to re-school her in a snaffle, and I don't think that David is going to manage to do it by himself.'

'I expect you're right,' said Noel, who didn't really approve of short cuts in schooling.

'I know it won't turn her into a dressage horse,' said Henry, 'but it'll give David slightly more control. At the moment he's a nuisance to everyone and a misery to himself. I think we've got a pelham put away somewhere. Elizabeth had a pony called Skylark which went in one. Remind me to ask Finch to have a look for it.'

'OK,' said Noel, and David said, 'Thanks a lot.'

Noel's ride were each having one last jump when the sound of hoofs was heard, and bits of Paulina and Eric could be seen through the shrubs which lined the drive.

'Time, gentlemen, please,' said Henry. 'The rally is now over and the meeting will begin without delay.'

'That's all very well,' said Christo; 'but I've lost my entire ride. They went up to the stable absolutely ages ago. Do you think I'd better go and look for them?'

'I'll go,' said Fanny, who was being the pony-less Marlowe. She had been on tenterhooks for some time wondering what her brother and sister were doing. Roly was a bad influence on Graham, she thought, as she set off at a run, and Deb was always hopeless.

'You're all very bright and early,' said Eric, looking round at the members and raising his eyebrows at the sight of Alex on Trappist.

'Yes, we've been putting in some extra schooling,' explained Henry.

'I really think I'd better go and look for those wretched kids,' said Christo. 'Honestly, they've been hours. I can't think what's happened to them.'

'We may as well all go up to the stables,' said Henry.

From the stable-yard they could hear high-pitched quarrelling voices in the orchard and Fanny was standing at the gate wringing her hands.

'What's going on?' asked Christo.

'I'm afraid they've let a few chickens out,' said Fanny apologetically.

'A *few*!' exclaimed Henry, looking at the mass of hysterically clucking white Wyandottes which were spreading across the orchard. 'Come out of there,' he shouted angrily at Graham, Roly and Deb, who were in the hen-run quarrelling over a feather and apparently quite oblivious of the open gate, escaping hens and Golly wandering loose with a foot through her reins.

'Are you mad?' Henry asked them. And Eric said, 'You kids are nothing but a downright nuisance.'

'It's my fault,' explained Christo hastily. 'I told them to get white feathers for the scavenger hunt, but I never dreamt they'd be so silly.'

'Well, come on everyone,' said Henry. 'We'd better catch them quickly or the club's reputation will be mud.'

'Can't these stupid kids catch them?' objected Eric. 'I don't see why the rest of us should waste our time chasing chickens. I mean to say, it's their fault and they should suffer for it.'

'It'll be me who suffers if they get in the garden,' observed Henry.

They spent a tedious twenty minutes catching the hens. Noel, Christo and Juliet caught by far the most. Henry, though speedy and active, was inclined to be left with bunches of tail feathers in his hand while his victims ran on. Eric was too dignified to run or grab; he stood about with a disgruntled expression on his face and got in everyone's way. Deb, Roly and Graham shrieked and chased the hens in the wrong direction; Fanny trailed after them wailing and scolding. David gazed at butterflies. Paulina was in the stable-yard brushing Starshine's mane. The last hen was the most tiresome. Thoroughly hysterical, she rushed headlong in every direction except the right one. Henry cursed, Christo tried to devise a plan of campaign, and Eric said that surely one hen wouldn't do any damage. Then Ruddy, his piggy eyes alight with excitement, came bounding on the scene.

He summed up the situation in a moment and, despite Henry's shouts, hurled himself at the hen. He caught her, held her for a moment, then she rushed on, her bulging crop protruding, pink and bare, while Ruddy spat out the white feathers which had covered it.

'That done it. Mother will be pleased to see a half-clad hen,' observed Henry.

David, suddenly becoming aware that he was supposed to be helping, flung himself on the unsuspecting hen, who had long ago decided that he was merely a stationary part of the countryside.

'Hurray,' shrieked Deb triumphantly.

'Thank goodness for that,' said Christo.

'Get down, Ruddy,' shouted Henry as Ruddy grabbed at the hen in David's arms.

'She looks rather fashionable,' said Noel when they had returned her to the run, 'like something out of the *Queen*. "Mrs

Wyandotte at the Radney Hunt Ball, wearing one of the new strapless dresses".'

'Don't you think it's time we stopped fooling about with chickens and got down to business?' asked Eric disagreeably.

'Can't we hold the meeting here, Henry?' asked Christo.

'Yes, I don't see why not. Let us retire to the less henny end and feast on apples as we argue,' answered Henry.

'Good egg,' said Roly. 'I'm *starving.*'

'Greedy,' said Deb, pushing him.

'If you kids can't keep quiet you'd better not come to the meeting,' said Eric angrily. 'You've wasted half the afternoon as it is, and I'm just about sick of you.'

The younger Marlowes and Roly looked slightly abashed and, when Henry had shaken down a shower of apples from one of the trees, they even offered the best ones to their elders. Despite the apples, the atmosphere of the gymkhana meeting remained tense. Henry, bored with the whole idea, allowed everyone to argue; he did nothing to stop the second string making silly suggestions, nor to soften Eric's crushing replies. When they had argued fruitlessly for quite ten minutes with Eric obstinately demanding a large show run on a grand scale and open to the world, Deb insisting that there must be dozens of events for people under ten, and Paulina inventing rules to keep out pot-hunters, Henry sighed heavily, sat upright and asked:

'What is the aim of this gymkhana?'

'Oh, gosh, must it have an aim?' asked Christo wearily.

'Couldn't it be in aid of some good cause?' suggested Paulina.

'I mean the aim or purpose,' explained Henry. 'Some horse shows are run to make money, some to draw a crowd, a few to encourage and improve a breed and fewest of all to amuse the competitors. What is ours going to do?'

'Amuse us,' shrieked almost all the members of the Radney Riding Club.

'Right. Then I suggest that each person thinks of the event he would like to have most. Personally, I think I'll be organizer and not enter – I'm tired of gymkhanas.'

'Oh, you can't be,' said Deb, looking at him in horror.

'He's trying to be funny,' said Roly firmly.

'Who wants what?' asked Henry, his pen poised over his notebook.

'Under ten, jumping,' shrieked Deb at once.

'Bending,' said Roly. After a lot of thought, Graham asked for a bareback trotting race.

'Touch and out jumping, no time limit, keep going until you bring a fence down,' said Eric.

'A Handy Hunter,' chose Christo.

'Musical Poles; everyone can enter for them,' said Paulina.

Juliet asked for an ordinary jumping class. David said that he didn't care – he was hopeless at everything. Fanny wanted Musical Poles, Noel an equitation test with jumps. Alex said that he had no preference.

'I regret to say that Musical Poles have the most votes so far,' said Henry, sucking his pen. 'I suppose we'd better vote on the other classes. Jumping under ten, for instance, how many people in favour? Roly and Deb. I'm afraid that won't make a class. Jumping fourteen years and under. How many people in favour?'

Alex, David, Fanny and Graham held up their hands.

'If we kept the jumps low Deb and Roly could enter too,' said Henry; 'and six isn't bad. Besides, we might get a couple of outsiders.'

'Let's make the Handy Hunter under eighteen,' suggested Christo. 'Then we can all enter.'

'And then Musical Poles,' said Paulina.

'The bending under fourteen.'

'What about something under twelve years?'

'The bareback trotting race sounds fun, it might be under eighteen.'

'What about the Equitation Test?'

'Why not a best-rider class?'

The meeting went on and on.

Henry lost interest again; he began to look up phrases in his French book. Noel and Christo peered over his shoulders.

'What are we going to say to him?' asked Noel. '*Bon jour, Monsieur le General,* is about as far as I shall get.'

'*Il fait tres chaud cet apres-midi,*' added Henry.

'*Combien de chevaux avez-vous?*' said Alex, after a short pause.

'I hope he won't have to shout "*faites attention a ce que je vous dis*" at any of us,' said Henry. 'He'd certainly cry, "*Prenez garde de tomber*" if he had to take the second string.'

'Translate, please,' said Alex. 'I like to know what is being said about me.'

'Take care not to fall,' said Henry, 'and the one before was "pay attention to what I tell you".'

'But supposing he comes to lunch?' said Noel. 'It's going to be terrible. Do your parents speak French, Henry?'

'No, at least they can't make intelligent conversation, which is what we want,' answered Henry.

'Let's learn three sentences each,' suggested Christo,' and then, with six or seven of us, there shouldn't be many awkward pauses.'

'But look at all the instruction that's going to be wasted,' said Henry. 'It is bitter to think that words of wisdom will fall on barren ground while our thirst for knowledge goes unslaked. There doesn't seem to be much horsiness in this book,' he continued in dissatisfied accents, 'except *"Regardez droit devant vous,"* which is what he'll shriek at Noel.'

' "My friend is a good judge of horses," ' read Christo over Henry's shoulder.

'That sounds conceited,' objected Noel. 'Besides, none of us is.'

' "What will you be occupied with tomorrow evening?" ' read Christo.

'Too inquisitive,' said Noel.

' "The more I go to France, the more I want to go there again," ' read Henry. 'Bags for one of my sentences. It's very polite, isn't it? And the French have a great love of the Fatherland, or is it the Motherland? *"Plus je vais en Français,"* ' he muttered. 'Here, Noel, do you want the book, while I commit this to memory?'

'Thanks,' said Noel, moving nearer to Christo so that they could both read.

' "Do you beyong to the Labour or Conservative party?" ' she read out. 'I say, that's a very woman-of-the-world question.'

'Do the French have Labour and Conservative parties?' asked Henry.

Noel sighed. 'It would *start* a conversation,' she said. 'He could then explain the differences between our countries' political parties – it would take hours.'

'And you wouldn't understand a word,' said Henry. 'No, thanks. I think we'll keep off politics.'

' "We thank you for your kindness",' read Christo. 'That'll do for your vote of thanks, Henry.'

'Secretary's job,' said Henry.

'Rot, absolute rot,' said Christo, becoming alarmed. 'It's the chairman's job and, anyway, your French accent is much better than mine.'

'Here are helpful remarks about the weather, morbid ones on the death of near relatives and sordid ones on discount,' said Noel, turning over several pages at once.

'Here, give me back that book,' said Henry. 'I've forgotten my sentence.'

'I thought we were having a meeting to discuss the gymkhana,' said Eric in a voice which shook with rage. 'I wouldn't have bothered to come all the way over here to chase chickens and listen to you airing your French accents.'

'But we're getting on quite well,' said Christo soothingly. 'Look, I've got the draft schedule written out. "The Radney Riding Club's first annual gymkhana",' she read.

| Class I | Handy Pony Competition | Riders under 14 yrs. |
| Class II | Handy Hunter Competition | Riders over 14, but under 18 yrs. |

Luncheon Interval

Class III	Jumping Competition	Riders under 14 yrs. Ponies under 14.2
Class IV	Jumping Competition	Riders under 18 yrs.
Class V	Bending Race	Riders under 14 yrs.
Class VI	Bareback Trotting Race	Riders under 18 yrs.
Class VII	Apple-and-Bucket Race	Riders under 14 yrs.
Class VIII	Musical Poles	Riders under 18 yrs.

'Those against the schedule please state their grievances without further delay,' said Henry as soon as Christo had finished reading.

'No Equitation Test, I'm going to sulk,' said Noel in a voice which belied her words.

'You know perfectly well that there's no one to judge it,' said Henry. 'Your objection, Miss Kettering, is frivolous.'

'I think it's unfair that there isn't a single event for people under ten,' grumbled Deb.

'You're utterly revolting – to put it mildly,' said Henry, fixing her with a scornful glare. 'Your one idea is to arrange the gymkhana so that you can win as many prizes as possible. If you can't control your competitive spirit you'll have to resign.'

Deb sat speechless; she gazed at Henry with her dark-blue eyes wide open and her mouth agape.

'Is it all right by you, Eric?' asked Henry, turning away from Deb.

'Yes, I suppose so,' answered Eric, sounding far from satisfied.

Henry was a jolly sight too high-handed, he thought, and he was always being so frightfully clever that you couldn't make out what he was getting at. Still, he had been pretty sharp with Deb.

'Yes, it's OK by me,' said Eric.

'There's only one thing left to decide, then,' said Henry; 'the judges. It seems to me that, as we've no class which needs vast experience or knowledge – no showing, no equitation, nothing that most of us couldn't judge ourselves, we might have youthful judges, and I was going to suggest that we ask a couple of the West Barsetshire people over to do the job. They know all about BSJA rules, Handy Hunters and gymkhana events, and it *would* be a relief not to have a grown-up to control.'

'Good idea,' said Christo enthusiastically.

'Well, you know them,' said Eric; 'but I must say there aren't many people of my own age I should care to be judged by.'

'Which West Barsetshires were you thinking of, Henry?' asked Noel.

'Susan, John, Dick,' said Henry.

'Well, would anyone like to suggest an alternative judge or judges?' he asked. 'Time is getting short, night is falling; Eric wants to get home,' he added when no one spoke.

'Oh, let's have your friends then,' said David, and everyone else seemed to agree.

'Good,' said Henry. 'I'll write to the judges, and Christo, you can write for the rosettes. There won't be prizes unless we get some outside entries or people persuade their relations to give them. I'm going to persuade my mother to give a challenge cup for the fourteen and under jumping.'

'I do wish it were under ten,' muttered Deb discontentedly.

'It looks,' said Henry, 'as though the meeting were over. And about time, too,' he added, before anyone else had a chance.

No one lingered to talk. The contentiousness of the meeting had left them all feeling vaguely dissatisfied with each other. Noel and Henry wandered to the house in dispirited silence. Letters had come for them by the afternoon post. Noel had read the postcard from her father and was opening her mother's letter when Henry thrust a typewritten letter at her. 'Look!' he said in excited tones. 'Just what we needed.'

The paper was headed 'Letchdale Dressage Group'. *Dear Sir, the above group is holding a novice one-day Horse Trial on 9 September,* read Noel, *and we wondered whether your Club would care to enter a team. We enclose full particulars –*

'We've got to enter,' said Henry.

'Let's have a look at the particulars.' Noel sounded doubtful. She thought that Henry was aiming much too high. How could *they* enter for even a novice Horse Trial?

'It just suits us. It's not as difficult as they usually are,' he told her cheerfully. 'A hunter trial course of one and a half miles, no fence over three feet six. A show-jumping course of ten jumps – none of them over three feet six. And surely we can ride a *novice* dressage test?'

'I don't think we're nearly good enough,' objected Noel. 'We'll make a hopeless mess of it.'

'Oh, don't be so *dismal*,' Henry told her. 'We've simply got to enter; it's our chance to make the riding club's name.'

Chapter 8

AFTER the arrival of the Letchdale Group's letter, living with Henry became very difficult. He refused to think about anything except the one-day Horse Trial.

'Curse the second string,' he said when Noel remarked that they needed some more tuition. 'Damn the gymkhana,' he answered when Christo asked him about printing and rosettes. He wakened Noel earlier and earlier each morning in an attempt to school before the flies became a nuisance and the day too hot.

Christo, the other member of the team, arrived at Radney Manor as early as she could manage, having done her walking exercise on the way over. Henry and Noel usually took their mounts for an hour and a half's walking exercise each evening. For jumping practice they arranged a course of low-spread fences and out for hacks they popped over any hedges or rails they could discover which could be jumped without damage to the farmer's crops. In between riding and schooling Henry was busy making and painting wooden markers and on the day General de Veriac's letter came he was marking out the arena with a tennis white-line marker.

General de Veriac had a tall, thin, spidery handwriting, and it took Noel, Henry and Christo, sitting on upturned buckets outside the saddle-room, some time to decipher it.

'Well, he's coming anyway,' said Christo, who had gathered the gist of the letter while the others were still stumbling over the first sentence.

'Thank heaven for that,' said Henry and, clearing his throat, he read:

' *"Dear Mr Thornton, – Thank you very much for your letter. I greatly appreciate the honour you have done me by your invitation to instruct the senior members of your riding club; I shall be most glad to do so. You ask me to name a day. Would Friday the 25th of this month be convenient for you? I decline, with many thanks, your kind invitation to lunch, for I have old friends near by to whom I will seize the opportunity of paying a visit: I shall be very glad, however, to accept your kind offer of tea. I am, of course, well acquainted with your good uncle, Major Holbrooke, and I trust that another meeting between us will not be long delayed. With kind regards, yours very truly, R. F. H. de Veriac."* '

'He writes terribly good English,' said Noel, with relief, 'and he's not coming to lunch. I don't think I'm going to learn any more French.'

'I must ring up Paulina and Eric and Juliet,' said Christo. 'Helen seems to have dropped out, but does she count as a senior?'

'Yes,' said Noel, and Henry answered 'No,' at the same moment.

'Well, I don't know, perhaps she is,' said Henry. 'She's paid her subscription, so I suppose you'd better tell her he's coming. I hope she doesn't come, though. She'll be a fearsome blot on the proceedings.'

'Tell her that he speaks very little English and is terribly ferocious,' suggested Noel. 'She didn't like being ticked off by Sanderson so she might think it safer to stay away.'

'None of us liked being "ticked off" by Sanderson,' said Henry. 'It still makes my blood boil to think of him. If this rally isn't a success I shall abolish the club, that's definite.'

'I shan't let you,' said Christo. 'After all, I'm an official too.'

'I'm giving Alex another lesson this morning,' Noel told them. 'I think he's lurking in Trappist's box now. I'll take him round in the far corner of the field, and you're not to come and look – it puts me off.'

'We shall be far too busy,' Henry assured her. Alex *had* improved. Noel felt quite proud of him. He no longer flapped his legs. He could canter out of a slow trot without his aids being obvious and he was sitting down very much better, too. She wished that Henry hadn't lost interest in the rest of the second string.

'We *must* practise them for the gymkhana,' she said at lunch. 'We don't want to horrify our West Barsetshire judges.'

But Henry only muttered, 'Curse the gymkhana.' Then, seeing Noel's disappointment in her face, he added:

'Look, you can teach them as much as you like, but honestly, I can't. I've simply got to get a hunter trial course organized, and I'm going to spend the next two days clipping jumping places in all the hedges in the district. I've mapped out a course.'

'I like hedge-clipping,' said Noel rashly, and condemned herself to clipping and hacking all through the long hot August afternoon.

The days between the arrival of the General's letter and his visit passed very quickly. Noel and Christo gave the second string two lessons, which included a practice for all the events at the gymkhana. The rosettes arrived, looking very smart with Radney Riding Club printed in gold on their cardboard centres, and Mrs Thornton drove into Waylebury and bought the *Thornton Challenge Cup.*

On Thursday afternoon and evening they tidied up the field

in honour of the General, and Henry marked out a new dressage arena. The second string and Juliet and Christo helped, and they were all quite merry except when Roly sat on 'C' and broke it. Juliet and Christo were sent home before everything was finished because they had to clean their tack – Finch had done Echo's and Sonnet's.

'I suppose,' said Christo, as she prepared to depart, 'that Eric and Paulina are lounging in their gardens. They *are* lazy devils; they jolly well ought to turn up and help.'

'Thank heavens they didn't,' said Henry. 'It's bad enough having certain members of the second string, but *they* would have been the end. Eric would have argued over every detail and I would have gone raving mad.'

'Paulina would have suggested ennobling causes, smiled sweetly on our tantrums, remained irritatingly clean and done nothing to help,' said Noel. 'She's worse than Eric.'

'Oh, *no*,' said Henry. 'She's irritating, but Eric's maddening.'

'Helen's worse than either of them,' remarked Christo. 'By the way, I rang her up, but I don't think she's coming.'

'Put out the flags!' said Henry.

When the work was done and the hot and dirty members had returned to their homes for baths and supper, Henry became dispirited.

'I hope that the General doesn't expect us to be any good,' he said. 'I hope he doesn't expect a huge number of people. I fear he's going to be sadly disappointed. We're going to have another flop; I feel it in my bones.'

'Oh, don't be so depressing; you're giving me the most terrible needle,' said Noel. 'I don't know the test properly yet,' she went on. 'Do you think he'll expect us to? Mind you tell him that we have only just started to learn it, and we've only practised it about six times.'

'He'll probably tell us that we can't possibly enter; that we're absolutely hopeless,' said Henry.

It rained in the night, but Friday morning was fresh and fair. The sun had lost some of its heat and the ground was not so hard; the leaves were less dusty, the grass greener and everywhere raindrops glistened in the sun. Finch was whistling cheerfully when Noel and Henry rushed out to the stable after breakfast.

'This is better weather for 'orses,' he told them. 'There won't be 'alf the number of flies about and the ground'll be riding better after that nice drop of rain.'

Sonnet seemed very cheerful; she whinnied hopefully and searched in both Noel's and Henry's pockets.

'Well, one thing is you don't have the needle,' remarked Noel, patting her.

'I bet Echo behaves like a maniac,' said Henry gloomily.

When they had carried out the garden table and a deckchair and placed them behind 'C' for General de Veriac's use, if he felt like judging the dressage properly, Noel and Henry found themselves with nothing to do. They visited the kitchen to inspect the cakes which had been made for the General's tea and then they hung about the stable-yard getting in Finch's way and imagining all the frightful things which might happen at the rally.

Christo was far too busy grooming Dragonfly to bother about the afternoon. The worst of black horses was the way they showed the dirt, she thought, as she water-brushed Dragonfly's croup in an attempt to make it look as clean and shiny as the rest of her. But still it was her favourite colour and it wasn't as tiresome as grey.

Eric strapped his ponies as usual, and put Choc-Bloc over the jumps. Then he ate an enormous early lunch and, telling his mother that he betted the old Froggie would make a far worse mess of running the rally than Colonel Sanderson, whatever Henry said, he retired upstairs to change into his second-best pair of jodhs.

Paulina caught Starshine with a great many loud and unnecessary cries of, 'Come up, old lady,' and 'Whoa, girl.' She gave her a perfunctory groom and, having embraced her several times, she wandered round the garden humming softly as she picked an armful of flowers which she arranged tastefully in vases and bowls about the house.

Juliet groomed Romeo and gave Roly some advice on his behaviour at the rally; he was not to play about with the Marlowes and he was not to make cheeky remarks in a loud voice.

At a quarter to two Henry, resplendent in his best breeches and coat, a pair of beautifully cleaned boots and a bowler, was waiting at the bottom of the drive. Noel, having put up the stile, which had fallen down, and placed a notebook and pencil on the judge's table, joined him. She was not so smartly dressed, for her only pair of jodhs were becoming rather short in the leg, but she was brushed and polished and she wore her crash cap and best tie.

Almost at once, Christo appeared on the scene and then Juliet accompanied by Roly on a bicycle. The rest of the second string arrived, on their feet or on bicycles, before the sound of Starshine's and Princess's hoofs was heard.

Henry sighed with relief. 'I was afraid that one of them might fail to turn up,' he explained, 'and five is such a miserable number.'

'I do wish we could ride,' said Deb. 'I think it's mingy keeping us out like this.'

'You know perfectly well that you're not good enough to be taught by de Veriac,' said Henry, and fixing her with a threatening eye, he went on, 'And you're to behave sensibly for once. If you start fooling or fighting you'll be turned out of the riding club, and I mean it.'

'OK,' answered Deb meekly.

'Hallo, what's the excitement?' asked Eric as he rode up.

'We're waiting for the General,' explained Christo.

'Well, you look pretty funny, I can tell you,' said Eric. 'You look as though there's been an accident or something.'

'Well, I'm not going to hang about here waiting for the old geezer; I'm going up to the field.' He rode on. Paulina, smiling sweetly on everyone, followed him.

'What's the matter with him?' asked Christo.

'Car,' yelled David, who had been aimlessly pursuing one of the more common varieties of butterfly.

'Coo! It's a swell bus,' said Roly as the long, black, shiny car approached.

'I bet it's him,' said Christo.

'I've forgotten the test,' said Noel panicking. 'I can't remember a word of it. Henry, you might tell me how it begins.'

'Don't be an idiot,' answered Henry crossly; 'of course you haven't forgotten it. Look, you rush and fetch Sonnet, then you and Christo can hold him in conversation while I fetch Echo.'

Juliet was already trotting up the drive towards the field, and the members of the second string had melted away into the shrubbery. Noel wailing, 'Oh, my needle,' and 'I'm sure that I shan't be able to think of anything to say,' fled in the direction of the stable-yard as the General's car turned up the drive. She had Sonnet out of her box and was in the saddle by the time Finch appeared.

' 'Ere, what's the 'urry?' he asked.

'The General's come,' gabbled Noel, preparing to ride away.

'Well, 'e won't want to see you with a tail bandage on and your girth loose enough to go round two 'orses,' said Finch. 'And you've been leaning up against them jumps; your coat's all white. Wait a minute while I get a brush.'

Noel tightened her girths while Finch was fetching the brush, and then she fidgeted with impatience while he brushed her coat and took off Sonnet's tail bandage.

'There you are,' he said. 'I'll bring Echo along.'

Deb met Noel in the drive. 'Oh, do be quick,' she shrieked. 'He's ever such an old, old expert and he's got white hair.'

'Don't yell so,' Noel told her; 'he'll hear.'

She trotted across the field to where the members were grouped together round the General. As Deb had said, he looked very old and he had a great deal of dazzling white hair. He was tall and thin, but he stooped a little and leaned on a black silver-topped cane. Henry seemed to be telling him about the Letch-dale Dressage Group's one-day event. The General was listening with all his attention.

He understands English, anyway, thought Noel.

'All right,' said General de Veriac, when Henry had finished speaking. 'We begin all together with our schooling. I correct you and then, later, we ride the test, yes?'

'That will be lovely,' said Henry. 'This is the sixth person,' he went on, pointing out Noel. 'Noel Kettering, General de Veriac.'

'How do you do?' said Noel as Henry hurried to take Echo.

'Very well, I thank you,' answered the General. 'This is a very nice pony that you have, young lady.' He patted Sonnet, who pricked her ears and looked smugly round at the other horses to see if they had seen that she was being admired. 'And your chairman also, he, too, has a very good mount,' the General went on, looking at Echo. Noel racked her brain for something to say, but she could think of nothing.

'We will begin?' asked the General, when Henry was in the saddle.

'Right-o,' answered Henry. 'Who's going to lead? Eric? Christo?'

Eric rode forward.

'If you will ride round outside the dressage arena ...' said the General. Eric led round, Christo followed him and then Henry, Paulina and Noel; Juliet brought up the rear.

'I will tell you "prepare to trot," and then "trot," ' said the General. 'You change the pace on the second command, you understand?'

'Yes,' answered Henry and Noel. The others made no reply.

He speaks very good English and he hasn't much of an accent, thought Henry, I wish I could speak French as well.

Christo felt the General's eyes upon her. He was looking at each member in turn. He had peculiarly piercing eyes, thought Christo, it quite gave her the jimjams to feel him looking at her.

He was a queer old bird, thought Eric, and he didn't look at all horsy in his posh chalk-striped suit. He needed a haircut too.

Juliet said, 'Steady, Romeo,' and tried to remember to keep her knees in. She did want to be a credit to Noel and Christo – they had spent such a lot of time teaching her.

Paulina thought, he'll notice me in a minute. After all, I have got the best seat even if I'm not one of these gymkhana-mad people. Colonel Sanderson soon spotted me. She smiled as she remembered that occasion and, giving Starshine a kick to keep her going, she began to hum softly.

Noel, trying to keep her eyes from the ground, was fussing about the test. She was certain that she had forgotten it. What did one do when one had changed the rein for the second time?

The second string and Finch had retired a little way back, and were sitting or leaning against the fir plantation railings. They conversed in whispers. Deb was insisting that the General was at least ninety. Roly put his age at seventy-four, and Graham felt certain that it was a concentration camp, not old age, which had turned his hair so white. David said that he looked like Einstein. Fanny, who had never heard of Einstein, thought he looked more like a musician and Alex said he was an elderly eagle. Finch said that he could tell he was a horseman by the way he had patted Sonnet.

The ride trotted and then cantered on either rein. After about ten minutes the General called them to a halt.

'Now,' he said, 'we have exercised our horses. That is important. The first rule of schooling; do not ask the horse for anything when he is first out of his stable. Ride him round, let him relax, let him again become accustomed to his rider's weight. Then, when he is exercised, we may start our schooling. Now, I have been looking at you with all my attention and, let me tell you, you are not too bad at all. You have faults, of course, but you do not ride too badly, any of you. Now, each one in turn, I will correct. First the leader. You, my friend, sit a little too far back. It is of paramount importance that one should sit in the lowest part of the saddle as near as possible to the pommel. Come forward,' he said, approaching Eric. 'Good, that is the position. Now the legs back a little and the reins a little shorter. It is good to ride with a long rein, but one must keep contact with the horse's mouth; one must not bring one's body forward over one's hands. The hands must be in front of the body and the shoulders back. You also,' he continued, advancing on Christo, 'are a soupçon too far back in your saddle, and you are too quick. Too quick to give your horse an order and too quick to correct him if he does wrong. You tell him, without warning. "Go," and, without warning also, "Stop." Now you must be progressive. You must tell him, "In a moment I will give you an order," prepare him and then apply the aids gently. It is possible to increase the severity of an aid if it is not at first obeyed. Do you understand me?'

'Yes, I think so,' answered Christo.

'Good,' said the General. 'And if he trots when he should remain at the walk do not be too sharp in your correction. With your reins tell him quietly that he is to walk. And this one,' said General de Veriac, turning to Henry; 'the big noise, the boss, whatever you call him, he is pushing his horse too much. He is a young horse?'

'Yes, five off,' answered Henry.

'His walk,' said the General, 'is not bad, but, all the time, you push, push, push. Your lower leg it never ceases to move. That is wrong. You should use your legs of course, but I may not see. I would have to be a blind man not to see yours. You must understand that it is too early yet to expect a very long step. You must keep him walking freely and up to his bit but if you try to go too fast you will get many short quick steps instead of the long swinging strides. If you push too hard, you will have him like that black mare there, her walk is too hurried. It is the same with the trot, the tempo must be slow and always even and quiet. This young lady,' said General de Veriac, turning to Paulina, 'she is the lazybones of the party. She sings a little song and enjoys the sunshine, but she does not work. Oh, no. She sits on her horse, this young lady, she does not ride him. Come now; forward in the saddle, legs back. Good. And we will see some work, please. These legs, that is what they are for. It must become a habit to ride one's horse always, but not to kick. That, let me tell you, is forbidden. It is press, press that we want. So.' He pushed Paulina's leg into Starshine as an illustration and then advanced on Noel. Feeling his eyes upon her, Noel began to blush, she fidgeted with her reins and looked at the ground. 'This one, she is a little stiff,' said the General. 'She must relax her spine and bring her shoulders back; so.' He pushed Noel into position. 'Now look up. Yes. And those hands, they shall follow the horse a little more. They shall keep contact with his mouth, but they shall also follow him. Bring them forward a little. Good. And this last one,' the General continued; 'she is more stiff. Her stiffness prevents her from sitting in the saddle at the trot or the canter. The stiff rider he goes into the air with every stride, but the supple one, he absorbs the movement of the horse and stays always in his saddle. Relax this back; put these shoulders back, so. Now we will see the seat bones on the saddle, please.'

When the ride was walking round again with everyone concentrating on curing his faults, the General called to them to prepare and then to halt. 'Now, look at you,' he said when they were standing still; 'the untidiness of it! You have stopped, perhaps, but you have not halted. Oh, no. You must halt with your horse at attention; yours – they sprawl. To halt one feels the reins, closes the legs, puts the shoulders back and increases the feel on the reins until the horse is ready to obey. But one does not pull, oh, no. The horse, he must halt straight, with his legs square and his weight evenly on all four of them. This business that you do; it is not riding. All right; walk on again and this time we will all do better.'

Noel's next halt was 'good,' Juliet's and Henry's were 'better,' but Christo's hands had been too severe, Eric had failed to close his legs and Starshine had looked like a 'ship without a sailor at the helm'. Twelve times the ride had to walk on and halt before everyone had done it well enough to satisfy the General. Then they were told to trot. When they had trotted round three times they were halted again and the General began by telling them that the trot was the pace at which most of the horse's early schooling was done.

'Concentrate on the trot,' he said, 'and when you have a good trot you will not be far from a good canter also. Now a good trot must be free and quiet. The tempo must be even, the horse must be balanced and appear to carry himself. Which among you, my friends, can boast a horse which fulfils each one of these conditions? The black mare? She has no tempo, she is not steady on her bit; always she argues with her rider, the hands of the rider must be steady. When the horse gives to the bit the hands of this one – how are you called?' Christo told him. 'The hands of this Mademoiselle Christo, they move and that is contrary to the principles of equitation. When the horse gives, we must reward him by giving also. We do not, mark you, throw away our contact, no, we lighten it. We maintain it by the weight of the reins but this Christo, when the horse gives, she takes, and that is wrong.

'And our leader, his mare, her mouth is wrong. It is her rider's fault. Too often he uses his hands and too rarely his legs. It is sitting in the wrong part of the saddle which gives him this fault, for it makes hard work of using the legs. This mare is frightened of her mouth. She will need a mild bit and much patient schooling. She must learn to lower her head and stretch out her neck at the walk; she must learn to accept her bit, to drop her nose and to stay steady on the bit at the trot. And the big noise, his horse it is coming, but he loses, sometimes, his tempo and his rider does not always keep contact with his mouth. You may ride with a long rein, Mr Chairman, your hands should follow, but, always, there must be a contact. The lazy one? She moves her hands and her legs. The hands must never move up and down; the legs, they must not look like the washing waving in the wind. Oh, no. The legs, they must remain close to the horse's sides and when we give an aid we press them into him. We do *not* take them a mile away and then thump him with them. That is not riding. The grey pony? Her trot is not bad at all. And this fellow? He is a bit of a lazybones. He does not use his hocks enough yet. You must push him on a little,' the General told Juliet. 'It is because you have not yet learned to use your seat bones and your legs, but he is a nice pony – he will learn.'

They trotted on again. Eric was feeling rather insulted. Princess, the winner of over a hundred and eighty rosettes, as good as told she was unschooled. It was fair cheek, but, of course, the old boy hadn't seen her in the ring. Paulina thought, he wants us all to take it so seriously, but if you can manage your pony and you don't fall off why does all this matter? Who notices how you halt your horse anyway, and I don't intend to work when I'm riding. I ride for pleasure.

Noel thought that Sonnet was going well. The rally was being a success. Everyone was learning lots and the General seemed quite agreeable. But she *still* couldn't remember the test.

'A slow trot sitting,' said General de Veriac.

And, Juliet thought, now I've got to relax.

'Do not bounce into the air, do not let the hand move up and down. Prepare to canter. Canter,' said the General.

Once round and they were called back to a walk again. 'This time we have a great lot of mistakes,' said the General. 'First, the horse must go quietly into a canter. He must not rush. He must remain straight, but he must go when he is told and not ten minutes too late when the dressage test is over. The rider, he must sit still. He must *close* his legs, not kick; he must *feel* his inside rein – not pull. He must not hang his head down to see what the legs of his mount do and he must not let his horse turn his head out nor his quarters in. We begin at the back end of the line this time. This young lady has so many mistakes that I must tell her quickly or I forget. You kick, you lean forward, you look down. Your horse continues to trot, then he decides he will after all canter; but you are leaning forward, your hands are forward – you give no rein aid at all. You understand that you should feel the inside rein?'

'Yes,' answered Juliet.

'But you do not do it. Make no mistake, you give the horse no rein aid at all, ' the General told her. 'He cantered on the wrong leg, he was unbalanced. You did not sit in your saddle, no. You look all the time to see which leg you are on and never do you make up your mind. Do I tell the truth?'

'Yes,' answered Juliet, smiling a little.

'The grey,' continued General de Veriac, 'she canters a little too fast and her rider does not sit down enough; that spine, it is too stiff. And the transition from the canter to the trot – it was not good – it was too sudden.

'The lazybones? She thought, this man, he does not know what he says. She gives a big kick. The horse falls into a canter, he is on the wrong leg – she does not notice – he is unbalanced – she does not care. A bicycle, it would do well for her. The big noise, Once again it is the trot that we must improve first; the canter, from out of nothing comes a severe aid. "Oy!" says our horse, "I do not like this," he swishes his tail – always a sign of resistance to the wishes of his ruler – he humps his back. He should go smoothly and cheerfully into the canter. The big noise must be more progressive; the horse, he must have more and more work at the trot.

'The black mare, she accepts nothing; neither the bit nor the legs, always she fights. She loses her tempo at the slow trot, she jumps into a canter and every moment she wishes to go faster. Once again it is the trot that we must improve first, the canter, it will come. But you must go quietly with this mare and make, each day, your aids a little lighter.

'And now our leader. He, also, will have to school his horse at the trot; she must learn to accept the bit. You see this mare, she has impulsion, she would go forward fast, but her rider prevents her; he is strong, that is how he holds her, but she is not schooled, so he cannot concentrate the impulsion beneath him and the horse does not go straight. She escapes from him sideways; at the canter her head turns itself outwards, the quarters inwards. This is a serious fault and there will be no merit in her canter while it remains.

'Now, before we start the test I have still one more point of importance which I would wish to mention. Corners; we meet many, many corners in our schooling and it is important that we ride them well. And I mean ride them, for we must not swing our horses round them as people who should know better sometimes do. Oh, no. We must never take a corner on two tracks; each one we must ride with care, it must be a half-circle and the aids for the corner are the same as for the circle. Make no mistake, my friends, there are many corners in a dressage test and each corner, it counts. The aids? Feel the inside rein, do not pull. Relax the outside rein, do not lose the contact. The outside leg closes behind the girth, the inside leg on the girth. The inside leg, he will prevent our horse from cutting the corner; he is of utmost importance. Right. We ride round at the walk and everyone see that he makes the half-circles.'

'And now,' said General de Veriac, when everyone was cornering to his taste, 'for the test.'

Henry at once began to explain that Eric, Juliet and Paulina had never seen, much less learned, the test yet and that he, Noel and Christo had only just begun to learn it, and they had ridden it only six or seven times.

'It is a good thing that you call me in,' said the General, grinning a little, when Henry had finished his explanation, 'for, let me tell you, riding the test is just what we should not do. Let this be understood: too much riding of the test is undoubtedly a bad thing. The horse learns the sequence of the movements, he begins to anticipate his rider's aids, and then we can rely on him no longer. No, when the postman brings our test we do not hurry to our arena and begin the practice, we sit, very serious and solemn and we analyse him. Can I have your test, please?'

'Certainly,' said Henry.

'Many thanks, now we analyse him,' said General de Veriac. 'First, we have two walks down the centre line and two halts facing the judges. The walk; we have ordinary walk and loose rein walk only. The trot; we have ordinary, sitting and extended. The canter is ordinary only, but there are two circles using half the arena. Now the transitions. From a walk into a halt, a loose-rein walk and an ordinary trot. From the trot into a canter. From an ordinary trot into an extended trot, from a canter into an ordinary trot. Now we have all these things to practise. We forget the test, we go into our arena or our school and we practise these things, in any order and at any marker. And the transitions we must practise many times, for they are important. Today we are going to ride our test in order that I may give you advice on which movements you make the most faults. But afterwards, remember, not too much test, for the horse will soon learn it by heart. The big noise, will he come first?' asked the General, walking towards 'C.'

'If you like, sir,' said Henry, 'but I warn you, I can't do it at all; my transitions will be nightmares.'

'He is a wise man,' said the General, sitting down; 'he makes his apologies before he begins. The other horses,' the General continued, 'they had better stand behind the jury. I am the jury,' he explained, when the members looked round vaguely.

Finch and the second string also gathered behind 'C' and then the General called, 'We are ready.' Henry, looking very grim and intent, entered at 'A' and tried to ride up the centre line to 'X.' Echo didn't walk very straight, in fact, he made a waving line of his own which criss-crossed and merged with the centre line at intervals. At 'X' Henry halted, rather crookedly, and saluted General de Veriac by taking off his bowler.

The General rose and bowed. 'Wait, I have something I wish to tell you,' he said as Henry prepared to ride on. 'To come in straight, you must look at something beyond "C." A tree, a post, a person – it does not matter – so long as it is in a line with and beyond "C." And do not hold the horse back so much; let him come forward. All right. You enter again.'

At the second attempt Henry's walk and halt were much better though they still couldn't be called straight. 'Seven,' shouted General de Veriac as Henry rode on after saluting. At 'M' Henry began to trot; at 'K' he changed the rein at the strong trot. General de Veriac was making notes. Noel was feeling slightly sick – her turn might easily be next. Henry was riding at an ordinary trot; now he had to change the rein again, another extended trot. At 'F' he returned to an ordinary trot and between 'A' and 'K' he slowed up to a walk.

Juliet was feeling certain that she would never be able to remember half of it and that she would do everything all wrong. I ought really to belong to the second string, she thought, I'm not nearly as good as the rest of the seniors. Eric yawned. It was child's play, he thought, any fool could walk, trot and canter at the different letters. Paulina thought that the rally was being very dull; the General was quite sweet but rather grouchy, and she allowed her mind to wander. She began to think of the white evening-dress which her dressmaker was creating in preparation for the teen-age dance at Waylebury in September. Christo was muttering the test as she watched Henry carry out the movements, in a last hasty attempt to commit it to memory. At 'H' a half-turn on the forehand. Ordinary walk to 'F,' another half-turn. At 'K' the walk became a loose-rein one. Dragonfly would certainly jog, thought Christo. 'H,' ordinary walk.

How on earth did Henry remember it all? At 'F' one cantered. Echo shot off with a buck, he changed legs, tried to change back again and became disunited. Henry pulled him up to a trot and restarted him. The cantering was quite easy to remember, thought Christo. Once round the arena and then a circle into a trot at 'E' then a change of rein. Sitting trot at 'K' and at 'F' one cantered, this time it was the near fore which led. Echo's second transition into a canter was better than his first; he only swished his tail and laid back his ears. The test was nearly over now, thought Christo, as Henry finished his second circle and broke into a trot at 'B.' She wasn't sure of this last bit. Between 'M' and 'C' one walked, and 'H' to 'K' was evidently a loose-rein walk. 'K' was ordinary walk again, at 'A' one came down the centre, at 'X' one halted, saluted and sighed with relief.

'Gosh,' said Henry as he rode out of the arena on a loose rein. 'I feel like a wet rag.'

'You find it difficult?' asked the General. 'But still, it was not too bad. I have here your mistakes. In the first ordinary trot you twice lost your cadence as you came into the corners. The transition to the extended trot, it was too sudden and there was not enough extension. To the ordinary trot – once again the transition was not good. The second strong trot, it was better and the transition to the walk it was quite good, but the walk itself, oh, no; it was terrible. The horse was not into his bridle, he wandered, he did not walk. And the rider's legs, they waved. Now, see here, all of you,' the General went on, taking hold of one of Henry's legs, 'it is not necessary to take the leg away from the horse to use it. It is not necessary, either, that we should move the leg backwards and forwards. The legs should always be close to the horse's sides; when we need them we press. Next came the turns on the forehand. It was not too bad, but in the first one you took two steps too many, you overturned him. The rein-back it was good, but a little crooked and there you halted and stood for a moment, but in this test you are not asked for a halt, but for an ordinary walk and, therefore, you must go straight into the walk without halting. Then the loose-rein walks. Well, you did not give him a loose rein. It is necessary to give him all the rein and to put your hands forward. An extended walk is ridden on a long rein, but always with a contact; and loose-rein walk is ridden on a loose rein with no contact, and the horse should stretch his neck out right down to the ground, if he so wishes.

'The canter, oh, dear, it was not nice to see. The transitions, they were not smooth and the circles they were ridden too fast. The finish was a little better. The general bearing of the rider was not bad, but the obedience of the horse was hesitatingly and not cheerfully given. His carriage still leaves much to be desired. But still, it will come. And here is your advice, so that you may read it later.'

'Thank you very much, sir,' said Henry. He sounded rather depressed.

'Mademoiselle Christo, will she go next?' asked the General.

Christo didn't know the test nearly as well as Henry and, with Dragonfly being rather difficult and refusing to come back to hand, she could not concentrate on the way, and she became rather muddled. The General, who said that he now knew the test, handed the document to Henry and told him to shout out the instructions at the appropriate moment.

'You see,' said General de Veriac, when Christo had finished, 'this mare is not quite ready to do the whole test yet. She needs more work at the walk and more still at the trot. Keep her very quiet and do not let her rein-back too quickly. She should go back quietly and smoothly.'

Then it was Noel's turn. She was thinking of the Horse Trial and whether the General would say that she, Henry and Christo were not good enough to enter.

'Go on, Noel,' shrieked everyone at once. And, realizing that the General must have told her to go next, she tore down to 'A' and hurried into the arena in a thoroughly flustered state. Sonnet jogged. Noel steered frantically in the direction of the centre line and gazed at the ground. She found herself at 'X,' stopped dead with Sonnet's legs far from squarely arranged. She bowed hastily and rode forward again. At 'C' track right, she recited and found that she could not remember which way was right and which left.

'What is the matter with you, young lady?' inquired General de Veriac. 'Have you to hurry home to tea?'

'No,' answered Noel, beginning to blush.

'Well, there is no need to hurry for me, I have no train to catch,' said the General. 'All right; go back; begin again, but more slowly and begin on the centre line, not to the left of him.'

Feeling very miserable, Noel turned and rode out of the arena. She was hopeless, she decided. Colonel Sanderson had thought so; General de Veriac was rapidly coming to the same conclusion. She might as well give up riding.

'Count ten slowly, and then enter,' said the General. Noel collected her thoughts and counted, this time she entered slowly, though she felt far from calm, and she found the centre line. 'Look up,' said General de Veriac as she rode towards 'X.' 'Look right over our heads.'

This time Noel remembered to halt slowly; she remembered which way was right and which left. Her confidence grew as she found that she hadn't forgotten the test. Sonnet turned on the forehand well; she rein-backed without any trouble. Noel remembered to send her straight forward into a walk. Now for the cantering. Sonnet was on the correct leg.

'Not bad at all,' said the General, when Noel had finished the test and returned to 'C' to hear his criticisms. 'The second entry, it was not bad at all. The ordinary trot, it was quite good, but it could be a little slower. The extended trot, it was not so good. We want more extension and the tempo must not be so much quicker than that of the ordinary trot – a little, perhaps, but not much. The turns on the forehand they were good, but a little quick. There is no hurry; this test, it has no time limit. You must try to keep cool and the horse, he must turn slowly, step by step. Never swing a horse; oh, no, to do so is not riding. The loose-rein walk, it was good, but there, once more, you must take care that the tempo is not too quick. It is the long step we look for, not the quick step. The rein-back, it was excellent; very nice and quiet. The sitting trot, there you were ambitious, you ask too much. This little mare goes very nicely, but her collection is not yet perfect; the test, it does not ask for collection, so do not try to give us what we do not want. The transitions into the canter, they were good, but the canter itself was a little too fast and also the circles. At the finish you turn late at "A" and once again you miss your centre line. It is necessary to turn a little before "A" in order that one may come straight down the centre of the arena. The horse, she carried herself well and was quiet and obedient, but the rider, she was in too much of a hurry and always she looks down.'

General de Veriac handed Noel the paper on which he had written his criticisms and, when she had thanked him, he asked if Eric would go next.

As Eric rode down to 'A' he did what he called waking Princess up. By giving her several sharp kicks and niggling with his reins at the same time he got her on her toes, and she jogged into the arena with her head in the air. Realizing that he was supposed to be walking, Eric pulled her up sharply and her quarters swung sideways. At 'X' he halted, rather crookedly, and then he began to niggle her legs into position as he did when called into the front line in the show ring. When he had her standing squarely he took off his crash cap. The General bowed over the table. Eric rode forward. At 'C' he tracked right, and it then became obvious to everyone standing behind 'C' what the General had meant about riding a corner as a half-circle. Eric and Princess certainly didn't. To keep Princess into her corners Eric had to pull the outside rein and this made her carry her head turned outwards. When he was in the corner, Eric let her turn and she swung her quarters outwards and took the turn on her forehand.

'You see?' said the General softly, and Henry, who was standing near him waiting to shout out the next movement to Eric, answered, 'Yes.'

'At "M" ordinary trot,' he shouted to Eric.

At the trot the fact that Princess was not straight became more noticeable and her cornering looked even more laborious. Her turns on the forehand looked quite good to Henry, but he thought that she reined-back too quickly and with her head too high. Her transitions into the canter were not smooth, and everyone could see that her circles were not true ones, for her body did not follow the curvature of the circle, and her head was flexed outwards instead of inwards. At the loose-rein walk Princess jogged and even when Eric persuaded her to walk she did not stretch out her head and neck. The General told Eric that it was of little use for him to criticize each movement individually as it was the basic training which was at fault.

'There is no use in building more and more storeys on bad foundations,' he explained. 'No. Go back; this is my advice to you, young man! Begin again with your schooling. Put this little mare in a snaffle, and teach her to drop her head and extend her neck. This one, she is afraid of her bit, but it can be cured and she is worth taking trouble over. Oh, yes, she is a nice pony.'

Juliet was the next victim. She moaned about being hopeless and not nearly good enough for a senior member, before she rode to the start, but Christo and Noel made heartening remarks, and Henry said that he would shout out the test especially loudly.

'You can see,' said the General quite soon, 'that this one she has not been riding so long as the rest of you, but she is not bad at all.'

Romeo was very calm and quiet, but he carried out most of the movements and transitions a little late, and he cut his corners. At the canter Juliet had the greatest difficulty to keep him in the arena, her circles were ridden too fast and they bulged in unexpected places. General de Veriac's criticisms were few but helpful. He said that her chief fault was not sitting down in her saddle, and that until she learned to do this she would not be able to use her seat bones, and therefore she would not be able to keep her pony balanced. He recommended that she should ride a great deal without stirrups and that she should practise the sitting trot, making sure that she relaxed her spine and kept her shoulders back. He pointed out to everyone that movements and changes of paces should be carried out when the rider's head and shoulders were level with the marker.

Paulina was called in last and, much to Juliet's surprise, it soon became apparent that she was the most hopeless of them all. Even with Henry shouting instructions at her, she seemed quite unable to carry out a movement in the right place. She could not keep Starshine in the arena and she seemed to have no idea how to change the rein. It did not look as though Starshine had ever been taught the turn on the forehand and the rein-back. And Paulina didn't notice when she cantered on the wrong leg.

'I say again,' the General told her afterwards, 'what I have said before; you do not ride, mademoiselle, you sit on your horse only, and to do dressage it is necessary to ride. You must ride in a school and you must practise these movements, for the whole reason for them is that they make the well-balanced obedient horses and the talented active riders. This cantering on the wrong leg it is not a serious fault if the rider shows he knows what he is about. He must stop the horse at once and restart him on the correct leg without delay. To make a mistake it is natural, but to canter all the way on the wrong leg, that is not dressage. Oh, no. Now, Mr Chairman,' the General continued, 'shall we each go through the test again with less mistakes this time? Have you the time or do you wish for your teas?'

'If you can bear it, sir, I for one, would like to do it again, very much indeed,' answered Henry.

'Same here,' said Christo.

'And me,' added Noel.

'All right,' said General de Veriac. 'In the same order then.'

Henry had profited by his own mistakes and those of others and his second attempt at the test was better, particularly in detail, than his first. Echo's worst fault, however, remained unchanged. He still lost his cadence when trotting round the corners. At the strong trot he still quickened his step rather than lengthened it, his transitions still lacked smoothness, his walk purpose and his canter was unbalanced.

'You see,' said the General when Henry had finished, 'it is not by riding the test that you improve the horse, but by the practice of the different movements and by schooling at the trot. By riding the test we improve the details and find what we have most need to practise. You do not learn at school by doing the examination again and again. No. You learn and practise a great many things, but only a few of them are asked for in the examination. With horses it should be the same. The dressage test it is not an end in itself, oh, no. It is to tell you if your schooling is well done.'

Christo's second effort was better too, but she said afterwards that riding the test on Dragonfly was like sitting on a volcano. You felt that she was likely to boil over at any moment and you hardly dared sit in the saddle, much less use your legs.

'Schooling, more and more schooling,' remarked the General. 'The mare's back it is not supple, she does not give her jaw; she is not at the disposal of her rider. You must ride many circles, Mademoiselle Christo. Ride them quietly and see that they are true circles; the horse quarters must follow exactly the track of his forehand. Also, you may practise the transitions from a walk into a trot and into a walk again. Ah, we have the young lady in a hurry,' said the General, seeing Noel preparing for her second attempt. 'All right, but slowly,' he called, signalling with a wave of his hand that she might enter. 'I will not fly away; it is very pleasant here in the sunshine.'

The second string, sensing that the atmosphere had become less serious, began to giggle. Noel could hear them, and she was scarlet in the face by the time she reached 'X'; however, she concentrated grimly.

'Do not scowl when you bow to me,' said the General becoming even more flippant. 'Ladies are expected to smile when they salute. It is not nice for the judge to be given the dirty look.'

The second string became quite hysterical at this. They were all, including Alex and David, bowing and smiling at each other in the most idiotic way and then subsiding into giggling heaps. Henry turned round and glared at them, and Finch said, ' 'Ere, that's enough of that.'

Noel was almost enjoying the test. She seemed to have much more time to think than at her earlier attempt, and she remembered to canter more slowly and to turn a little before 'A' for the last ride up to 'X.' She even managed to give a faint smile when she saluted at the end.

'Good,' said General de Veriac. 'Yes, this time it was good. It is the extensions and the transitions which you must practise.'

To everyone's surprise, Eric seemed quite keen to try the test again and when he had finished Juliet had another attempt.

Paulina said that she didn't really think there was much point in her doing it again.

'I'm not good enough,' she said in a reproachful voice. 'I don't want to keep everyone waiting about.'

'What does she say?' the General asked Henry. 'If she wishes it, we have time, but if she does not care to try again, we will have tea. I do not mind.'

Henry gave Paulina a ferocious glare, but she only looked even more of a martyr, and so he told the General, 'I don't think she does want another try.'

'Well,' said the General, rising, 'I would not let the young lady who is in a hurry send me before, but now I am ready, and at tea we will talk more about the test – the one-day event. Yes?'

'If you think,' said Henry, handing Echo over to Finch, who had hastened forward, 'that we're anything like good enough to enter.'

T–D

Noel and Christo, who had both been haunted by that very fear all afternoon, rode nearer to hear the General's answer.

'But, yes,' he said. 'You will be all right to enter. Your dressage is not yet good, but you will not be by any means the worst there. You are not bad at all in comparison with many of the competitors I have seen in English dressage tests. You must not be downhearted by my criticism. Always one can criticize, especially a novice dressage horse, for ten out of ten is perfection and that is not reached in many movements. Oh, no.'

Henry stopped for a moment to tell horse owners that they could borrow loose-boxes and help themselves to hay and to ask Noel to bring everyone including the second string into tea. Then he took the General into the house, answering his questions on the various horses' and ponies' jumping ability on the way.

Except that Graham ate most of the egg sandwiches, and Alex broke a plate, everyone behaved excellently, and the tea passed off gaily. Mrs Thornton appeared for a few moments and was introduced to the General, and then she returned to her bridge party in the drawing-room. Mr Thornton could not be found. The General was very agreeable, he talked to almost everyone and gave the senior members a great deal more good advice. All the members were there to see him off and they all thanked him for coming a great many times.

As he shut the door of the long shining car, he reminded them, 'Aim to be there one hour before you are wanted, and ride the horses for half an hour before the test in order that they shall be loosened up and supple. Ride them quietly and let them become used to their surroundings.'

'Well, thank you again for coming,' said Henry. 'We've spent an enjoyable as well as an instructive afternoon, and we really are most grateful.'

'It is nothing,' General de Veriac answered him. 'It was a pleasure to find myself among such enthusiasts. Good luck to you and au revoir. I hope I may be there to see you perform.'

'That was a progressive move off, if you like,' said David, gazing after the retreating car. 'I bet he's a jolly good rider.'

'He was quite a decent old geezer,' said Eric in patronizing tones.

'Awfully nice,' agreed Christo.

'He could teach too,' said Henry.

'I learned masses,' added Noel.

'Much better than silly, stupid sodden Sanderson,' shrieked Deb.

'Up with Veriac,' bawled Roly.

'Oh, that was right in my ear,' said Paulina crossly. 'Why can't you behave properly? You're so rude and noisy.'

Deb giggled and David murmured something about proper, peevish Paulina.

'I think I'd better be going,' said Eric, giving the younger members of the second string a contemptuous look.

'What's the time?' asked Alex.

'A quarter past six,' answered Henry.

'Oh, goodness, come on, Roly. We shall be late for supper,' said Juliet.

'I must do a bunk too,' said Christo.

They all walked in the direction of the stables. Henry began to talk about their future schooling. Christo said that she would come over next day. The bicycling and walking people helped to saddle and bridle the ponies, and then everyone left at once, calling 'Good-bye,' and 'Thanks awfully for the tea,' as they disappeared down the drive.

'We'd better muck out some of these boxes,' said Henry to Noel. 'Finch is still here, but it's long after his usual time.'

'OK,' said Noel.

Chapter 9

'AND now,' said Christo on Saturday morning, when they had finished discussing General de Veriac, the rally and the new things they had learned, 'we've got to think about the gymkhana.'

Henry groaned, and then said, 'Well, we're not going to slack off the schooling, so don't you think it. In fact, we've got to work harder than before, now we know what's wrong with us. The reputation of the club is at stake.'

'The reputation of the club will be mud if we run a gymkhana which is a complete flop,' Christo pointed out, 'and time's getting short.'

'Oh, why did I ever agree to holding a gymkhana at all?' wailed Henry.

'The second string have got to have *some* fun,' said Christo, 'and, personally, I like gymkhanas,' she added defensively.

'Oh, gosh!' said Noel, suddenly awakening from a reverie. 'Henry, I'm terribly sorry, but I told Alex I'd give him a lesson at eleven-thirty today. Is that all right?'

Henry groaned again. 'I suppose so,' he said; 'but we'd better start schooling at once or we shan't fit in an hour.'

'You and I can discuss the gymkhana while Noel takes him,' said Christo.

They agreed that it would be best for them to school separately, and try to improve the faults which the General had pointed out, then, at the end of the lesson they would each perform in turn for the inspection and criticism of the other two.

They had not been riding for very long when there was a loud shriek from Henry. Noel and Christo left their corners of the field and rode across to him.

'What's the matter?' asked Christo.

'It was a cry of horror,' he explained. 'Your chairman has committed an unpardonable error. He has thrust important club correspondence unopened into the pocket of his best riding-coat and forgotten all about it.'

'What correspondence and how long ago?' asked Christo.

'And then you say I'm always in a dream,' remarked Noel.

'It was yesterday morning,' said Henry, 'and they looked suspiciously like communications from the West Barsetshire people and my Uncle G. Here, hold Echo, someone.'

Noel took Echo because he knew and liked Sonnet, and Henry ran off at full speed. He soon reappeared clutching three letters. He gave one each to Noel and Christo. 'I'd better have Uncle G's,' he said, 'just in case he's being uncle-y.'

They tore open the letters and began to decipher them.

'Mine's from somebody called Dick,' said Christo. 'His writing is so jolly small and niggly that it's almost impossible to read, but he seems to be coming.'

'Mine's written by John, I know his writing, it's very large and solid, but it's a joint answer from him and Susan, and they're both coming,' said Noel.

'Lord!' said Henry. 'We're going to have a houseful. What is Mother going to say? Uncle G's letter isn't very interesting,' he went on, 'except that it contains a few biographical notes on the General. He seems to have won the Grand Prix dressage championship of Europe three times and to have show-jumped everywhere. Good thing we didn't know before, we should none of us have dared open our mouths to him. Here, Noel. Do you want to read it?' He chucked the letter at her.

'He is lucky,' said Noel, when she had finished reading the letter. 'I wish I could go to horse shows in France and Belgium.'

'Well, we've got the judges and the rosettes and the schedules, so we're getting on,' said Christo.

'I've got to square Mother,' said Henry. 'I'd better have a go at lunch.'

At the end of an hour's schooling, Christo, Noel and Henry found each other very much improved, though they were still by no means perfect at riding up the centre line and halting straight, which was one of the movements they were practising.

Fortunately, Alex had also developed the improvement mania and he didn't object at all when Noel, seeing him through new eyes, began to cure a hundred faults of which she had never noticed the existence before. In fact, he insisted on practising halting from the walk for a quarter of an hour, during which Noel became rather bored. They finished the lesson with some jumping. Alex was riding with much more dash and determination, so Noel let him jump the wall. He fell off at the first attempt, but, remounting quickly, he had another try and this time he was safely over.

'Couldn't I have a try at the hunter trial course?' he asked when Noel began to arrange an in-and-out for him. 'It looks most awfully tempting and I don't mind a bit if I fall off.'

'What about my nerves?' asked Noel. 'I don't think they'll stand it. Besides, we'll have to ask Henry as it's his pony and his course.'

Christo and Henry had retired to the morning-room. In an attempt to be businesslike Christo had seated herself at the table, but Henry was sitting astride a chair at the other end of the room and, as he talked, he tilted it.

'I've brought a schedule for you and one for Noel,' said Christo, 'and I've posted or delivered one to each of the club members and sent a few to strangers who, I thought, might be interested. There are quite a lot of people with ponies of their own on the other side of Waylebury, but they're mostly rather young. Now, can you think of anyone else who'd like one? We don't want the Ridgeways, do we?'

'No, I don't think so,' said Henry. 'They're rough, they ride badly and they're awfully professional. Dad would probably chase us with whips if we refused. Oh, I say, what are we going to do if Daddy Lawson starts interfering?'

'The chairman has to deal with him,' answered Christo. 'Now, look, do you want some schedules for the judges?'

'Oh, lord, yes,' said Henry. 'I'd forgotten all about them, and I'd better have their badges too.' He got up and came to the table. 'I say, I'd no idea we were so grand,' he said, picking up a schedule. 'Who printed them?'

'Daddy's office has a sort of tame printer who does all their work,' explained Christo, 'so I wangled this in with everything else. I thought we might as well have them done for nothing.'

'Wonderful,' said Henry. 'They look absolutely first rate. I must say, Christo, you're a marvellously efficient secretary.'

'Oh, yeah,' said Christo, 'until everything begins to go wrong. What about these numbers? Do you think they'll do?'

'Well, they're obviously amateurish,' said Henry; 'but I've seen much worse. Who made them?'

'David Rice-Greene,' answered Christo. 'He paints a bit, I believe and he said he could do lettering. He's doing some notices now. You know, *To the Gymkhana* – with an arrow, and *Collecting Ring*.'

'He's quite an acquisition,' said Henry, 'compared with most of the second string.'

'Well, so far, we've only spent twenty-five shillings,' said Christo, 'so it looks to me as though we shall be able to give all the entry fees back in prizes, unless we have to hire the rope for the ring. But Daddy's seeing someone on the County Council about borrowing its supply of rope.'

'We've got plenty of stakes,' said Henry. 'There's a huge pile down by the greenhouse. And we've got a megaphone, but we shall need someone with a loud voice as collecting steward.'

'Well, actually,' Christo told him, 'Gerry and Bill have already offered to manage that side of it for us. They're disgustingly electrically minded and among their gadgets they've got a home-made mike; Gerry thought that he could be collecting steward and Bill electrician.'

'That would be perfect,' said Henry.

'They offered to install field telephones too,' said Christo; 'but I didn't think we needed anything quite as complicated as that.'

'No, but they'd be grand if we ever had hunter trials,' said Henry. 'We still need people to put up jumps and someone to be secretary on the day,' he went on. 'You won't want to be giving out numbers, taking down results and seeing that the judges get the right prizes and rosettes if you're riding.'

'No, couldn't someone's mother do that for us?' asked Christo.

Henry didn't agree. 'No, let's keep grown ups out of it,' he said.

'Well, we'd better rack our brains and ring each other up,' said Christo. 'I must dash now. I swore I'd be back to lunch. We've got a river expedition on this afternoon.'

'Lucky wretch,' said Henry. 'Think of Noel and me riding under a sweltering sun. I wish we had some decent woods round here.'

'Put it off till the evening,' advised Christo.

'Can't. We're going to the theatre; there's a very good company doing Shakespeare at Swyncombe.'

On the Tuesday before the gymkhana, Noel organized a last practice for the second string. They began by schooling. Every-one seemed improved and Noel's spirits rose. But, when they started to practise the gymkhana events, the riders appeared to be paralysed by fear or the needle. In the bending race they either missed out posts, failed to go faster than a trot or gal-loped round the field out of control. Tanzy, who had been be-lieved cured of her careering habits by the Thornton vulcanite pelham and standing martingale, was worse than ever. Christo told both David and Alex that they were 'too feeble for words'.

The Marlowes complicated matters by being perpetually on the wrong pony for the event which was being practised and, when they changed ponies they had to change stirrups, which took a very long time. Juliet added to the confusion by offering to lend Fanny Romeo for the Handy Pony and the Apple and Bucket race. Fanny was delighted; she said that she had never ridden such a wonderfully smooth pony in her life. Deb was very jealous; she muttered that Fanny was getting too grand to ride Golly, but that she betted Golly would beat Romeo in the Handy Pony. Christo, who overheard this remark, caused great consternation by saying:

'Unless you all ride a jolly sight better than you're doing to-day, I can't see any of you winning anything. We've six outsiders in Class I and at least three in all the other classes.'

Those members of the second string who had been imagining their stable walls decorated with rows of rosettes gave faint cries of horror.

'Oh, why did you let them enter?' demanded Deb.

'Are they good?'

'Who are they?'

'They'll win *everything*.'

'It's no fun winning if there's no competition,' Christo pointed out.

'And it's bad for your characters,' added Noel.

At the end of the lesson the instructors gave their pupils a few last instructions.

'Now, mind you all clean your tack decently,' said Christo. 'Some of it doesn't look as though it's been cleaned for months, and it'll ruin the riding club's reputation.'

'And for goodness' sake keep your knees in,' said Noel; 'we don't want corpses all over our show ground.'

'What are you Marlowes going to do about Golly's mane?' asked Christo. 'You can't come with it like that. Is it meant to be long or hogged?'

'Well, we don't know,' explained Fanny. 'You see, I want to have it long, Deb wants it hogged and Graham won't say.'

'I should hog it,' advised Christo. 'It'll be dreadfully thick and untidy if you do grow it.'

'There, I told you so,' said Deb triumphantly.

'All right,' said Fanny, ignoring her sister, 'and we'll plait Swansdown's.'

'Noel, for goodness' sake show me how to plait,' said David in a hoarse whisper. Grumbling about the thickness of Tanzy's mane, Noel showed him. Christo showed Fanny.

'Deb, you're not to jump Golly any more between now and

the show,' said Noel. 'If you do, you're certain to have three refusals and disgrace the riding club.'

'Put your knees in, Graham,' shouted Christo, as everyone began to move towards the field gate.

'What about me, Noel?' asked Alex. 'Am I having another lesson before the gymkhana?'

'Yes. What's today?' asked Noel. 'Tuesday, isn't it? Well, it'll have to be tomorrow then. We don't want to make Trappist stale by jumping him the day before.'

'Good-bye, all,' said Christo. 'I'm going to school Dragonfly now. I'm still reeling from yesterday's circles,' she told Noel.

It was obvious from the very beginning of the gymkhana preparations on Thursday afternoon that everything was determined to go wrong. The mallet, the property of the Thornton family, broke, almost with the first blow, leaving eight pairs of posts for jumps and a legion of ring-rope stakes to be knocked in. Henry left Christo and Noel in charge of the second string, and departed to Waylebury on the next bus to buy a new mallet. At first everyone was very active. Alex rushed home and fetched a huge coal-hammer with which he and Christo began to knock in posts. David, who was in charge of notices and flags, and had borrowed flags from all round the district, was rapidly transforming the grounds of Radney Manor. Noel, Juliet and Fanny began by putting the jumps which didn't need knocking in into position and then they collected and sharpened bending poles. Graham bicycled home to find some buckets for the Apple and Bucket race. Christo sent Deb and Roly to whitewash the stile. Eric and Paulina had, so far, failed to appear.

For a time everything seemed to be going well and then Noel, looking up from her maddening task of trying to persuade reluctant bending poles to stand up, realized that very little had been accomplished and that it would soon be tea-time. Juliet and Fanny were standing and talking, Deb and Roly were shrieking their heads off – she supposed they were doing something tiresome. Alex was sitting in the shade and grumbling about the heat. Graham hadn't returned and David was nowhere to be seen. Suddenly Fanny stopped talking and sprinted across the ring.

'Deb, Deb, stop it,' she cried. 'Oh, Deb, how can you?'

Everyone turned to see Deb and Roly rolling about on the ground hitting each other with whitewash brushes. At that moment Roly hit Deb a hefty blow on the head and she started to cry, making her usual ear-splitting noise.

'Oh, shush,' said Fanny. 'Deb, do be quiet. Everyone will hear. And just look at the whitewash you've wasted.'

Deb roared louder than ever. Noel stood by feeling very helpless; she wasn't used to the tantrums of younger brothers and sisters. Juliet was lecturing a scowling, red-faced, whitewash-bespattered Roly when Christo joined them.

'Horrid little beasts,' she said. 'Shut up, Deb, you're deafening us.'

'Oh, dear, just look at your jodhs,' said Fanny, 'and you're supposed to be riding in them tomorrow.'

'You'll be a disgrace to the club,' said Christo crossly, 'as well as wasting all its whitewash. Honestly, if you two don't behave sensibly I shall tell Henry to chuck you out. You're always making a nuisance of yourselves.'

'What are we going to do about all this whitewash just in front of the jump?' asked Noel. 'It's enough to put any horse off. I can see we're never going to be ready in time,' she went on in depressed accents, 'everyone wanted to have a show, but hardly anyone will help to do the work.'

'Earth,' said Alex, suddenly realizing that he was one of the people not doing any work. 'We can sprinkle some earth on top of the whitewash, that'll hide it,' he said. 'At least Deb and Roly can, as they made the mess.'

'Good idea,' said Christo. 'Go on, you two, and no more squabbling.'

'Do you think those posts look all right?' asked Noel pessimistically as she surveyed the layout of the ring. 'I don't see how we're going to fit all the jumps in. That corner looks too sharp to me.'

'Oh, rot,' said Christo. 'There's tons of room. Don't be so dreary, Noel. Besides, we can't possibly start pulling them all up now.' At this moment they heard a shout and turned to see Henry striding across the field carrying the new mallet over his shoulder.

'Gosh, she's a weight!' he said, dropping it as he joined them. 'How are you getting on?'

'Not at all,' and 'O K,' answered Noel and Christo at once.

'Well, we've knocked in a good many stakes with Alex's coal-hammer,' said Christo.

'If you ask me, we're never going to be ready,' said Noel. 'The whitewashing people have merely made a frightful mess. The bending poles won't go into the ground, much less stand up and I don't see how we're going to fit eight jumps in a ring that shape.'

'Cheer up, take courage, you confirmed pessimist,' said Henry gaily. 'It doesn't get dark till ten.'

'Here, I want to go to bed early,' objected Christo.

'And we've got to be home by seven,' said Juliet.

'To work,' said Henry. 'Where have you got to, Christo? I'll do some bashing in now.'

'Well, that's the entrance over there,' said Christo, pointing. 'Supposing you began from the other side, I'll carry on too, and we shall soon meet.'

'I'll start putting the rope round,' said Alex.

'Here's Graham with dozens of buckets,' said Juliet. 'And Eric; oh, good, he's strong.'

When Alex had fixed the ring rope round all the stakes which had been knocked in, it became obvious to everyone that the ring was both a strange shape and too small.

'No one,' said Eric, who seemed to have appointed himself inspector of the course, 'could jump that wall at that angle and the gate's much too close, but if you move it any farther away it'll be on top of the parallels. I mean to say, you can't get away from it, the ring's much too small.'

'And we've got to fit in the in-and-out for the Handy Hunter,' said Henry. 'It's obvious that we shall have to pull up a few stakes. Sorry, Christo.' The 'few' stakes which they pulled up seemed to Christo to be almost every one which she and Alex had knocked in at such expense of time and energy.

'We might as well have sat in the shade all afternoon,' she remarked bitterly.

'Christo, you might come and see if *you* can get these beastly bending poles to stay up,' said Noel.

Feeling much too hot, but very virtuous, David, having arranged every flag and notice in a suitable spot, came into the gymkhana field expecting to find most of the work done. One glance told him that all was not going well, and then he observed Roly, Deb and Graham practising the apple and bucket part of the Apple and Bucket race beside the water-trough. They were soaking wet and they looked marvellously cool.

'Why don't you do some work?' he demanded. 'It isn't fair that you three should spend the whole afternoon amusing yourselves while everyone else works.'

'Quite right,' said Alex. 'Come on, you lazy devils.'

'Mind your own bally business,' said Roly.

'Ready, steady, go,' yelled Deb, and they began another race. Alex and David threw themselves on Roly and Graham, and knocked them over, Deb rushed to Graham's aid and attacked David from behind. The noise soon attracted the attention of the labouring senior members. 'Stop it,' they yelled, and, 'Why don't you come and do some work?'

'I'm never going to run a gymkhana for the ungrateful little beasts again,' said Christo crossly.

'I thought you wanted the gymkhana too,' said Henry. 'You said that you liked them.'

'Well, I don't like knocking posts into ground like concrete on the hottest day of the year,' said Christo furiously.

'Your knocking in doesn't seem to have done much good,' said Eric tactlessly. 'I mean, we're barely half-way and it's tea-time.'

'Well, if you'd come a bit earlier or Henry hadn't gone dashing off to Waylebury we might have everthing done by now,' said Christo. 'It's easy to turn up at the last minute and criticize everyone else for not having done more.'

'That's what you think' said Eric angrily. 'I came as early as I could. I haven't got all day to waste up here even if you and Henry have.'

' "If you can keep your head when all about you are losing theirs and blaming it on you",' quoted Henry in an irritatingly detached voice, and he began to knock in the posts for the triple.

'I feel like having a nervous breakdown and varicose veins,' said Noel.

When all the posts had been knocked in, Henry announced a short interval for lemon squash and cake, after which everyone felt much more agreeable. They decided that they would have to use a crowbar to make holes for the bending posts, and white-wash to mark each hole, so that they could put up the posts quickly. For, as Henry said, they didn't want half an hour's wait between the end of the senior jumping competition and the beginning of the bending.

At ten minutes to seven the ring was ready; the jumps were in position, the bending poles, the buckets and apples were ready at the ringside.

'People who've got to be home by seven had better go,' said Christo.

'Come on, Roly,' said Juliet, and the Naughtons and Marlowes disappeared at full speed. David wandered after them, and Eric said that he supposed he had better be getting along.

'What now?' asked Noel.

'We've got to decide the Handy Pony and Handy Hunter Competitions,' answered Henry. 'Got any writing paper, secretary?'

Christo found her coat and handed him a pad and pencil.

'Handy Pony Competition, riders under fourteen years,' read Henry. 'Now, are we going to have any jumping in it?'

'Yes,' said Alex.

'No,' said Christo. 'At least Mrs Landon, whose tiny tots are entering, rang me up, and I told her that there wouldn't be any – you see they're only six – but I said that they would probably have to lead their ponies over a tiny jump.'

'It'll have to be a really low jump,' said Henry, 'or they'll trip and break their necks. One isn't exactly competent at six, is one?'

'What about a garden path?' suggested Noel.

'And reining-back between posts,' said Christo.

Henry was writing rapidly. 'I think reining-back without posts,' he said. 'I've seen little dears trying to do it between posts before; it takes hours and it's most frightfully dull. Can't we just say "halt at the red flag and rein-back four steps"?'

'No flags left,' said Christo. 'David bagged them all for his decorations.'

'We can take one down. The place looks like the home of the United Nations, anyway,' said Henry.

'What about using the dressage markers?' suggested Noel.

'Do they all know the alphabet?' asked Henry.

'Here, I'm in this class,' said Alex indignantly.

'Lucky you,' said Henry. 'You'll probably win it.'

'I'm in favour of dressage markers,' said Christo.

'O K,' said Henry. 'Well, that's enough for them to do; we don't want to overtax Alex's brain. Look, you read this through and see if you think it's all right, while I knock some dressage markers in at the appropriate spots.'

When the Handy Pony test was settled they discussed the course for the Handy Hunter. Henry complained that they had no gate to open and shut.

'We don't want it to degenerate into a sort of scurry race,' he said. 'We must test the handiness of the hunters.'

'We can use the triple for slip rails,' said Christo. 'I mean the taking down the top bar and leading your horse over the lower one affair.'

'And we've got the right-angled in-and-out,' said Noel.

Henry, however, wanted something original, and while the others discussed the heights of the jumps for the two jumping competitions, he continued to think. The second string's course was very complicated owing to the gate, wall and brush all having to have substitutes as they were too big for the small ponies. Christo said that she understood the course and would be head steward for that event, but Alex, being the eldest of the second string, would have to be in charge of the stewarding for the senior jumping competition. Alex said that he was sure to do it all wrong and that David would be much more efficient, but Christo merely told him not to be weak.

Suddenly Henry interrupted. 'Got it,' he said. 'A strand of imitation barbed wire fixed across the stile. Competitors have to pull up, take it down, before they can jump the rest of the stile. If your horse won't stand for you to unhook it he isn't handy and deserves to waste time.'

'Good idea,' said Christo.

And Alex said, 'I've got some silver paint at home, so I'll make the wire, if you like.'

'That would be perfect,' said Henry.

The bending and the trotting races were easy to arrange.

'We can steward for the bending,' said Henry; 'but I don't quite know who's going to clear away the poles and arrange the three buckets at the far end of the ring for the trotting people to turn round, practically everyone seems to have entered.'

'Alex hasn't,' said Christo. 'Nor Fanny, nor that damp Paulina.'

'Alex is in charge of that, then,' said Henry. 'And after that I've finished riding so I'll take over for the last two classes. I haven't entered for the Musical Poles, they bore me.'

'I haven't entered for anything except the Handy Hunter and jumping,' said Noel. 'I'm much too afraid of undoing my schooling to ride in gymkhana events just before a dressage test.'

'Well, Dragonfly's so scatty, anyway,' said Christo, 'that I've thrown caution to the winds and entered for everything.'

'You are an idiot,' Henry told her. 'She'll be hotter than ever.'

'You're always saying that dressage improves horses,' said Christo; 'but I can't see any point in improving them if you're going to give up entering for practically everything. Besides, gymkhana events don't bore me yet.'

'Of course, a dressage-trained or well-schooled horse is better at everything,' said Henry; 'but Dragonfly has hardly begun to respond to her training yet. She isn't calm, obedient or well balanced and therefore she isn't really fit to be raced and hotted up, any more than Echo.'

'Fusspot,' said Christo.

Henry shrugged his shoulders. 'She's your horse,' he said.

They discussed the music for the Musical Poles. Record players, they agreed, were hopeless as they were always inaudible on the far side of the ring. Christo suggested that a whistle should be the signal to gallop in; Alex, that a car horn would make more noise, but Henry's suggestion of a hunting-horn – he could blow one vaguely, he said – was adopted in the end.

'Well, everything really is settled now,' said Henry, 'and, as long as the assistant secretary and the collecting steward can read our writings, our organization should be O K.'

'Angela's very efficient,' said Christo; 'but she's not at all horsy. I don't think she's ever been to a gymkhana in her life. She's going to do secretarial work when she leaves school, so I told her that this would be good practice for her.'

'Being secretary on the day is a fearfully dreary job,' said Henry. 'She'll probably never forgive you when she discovers what you've let her in for.'

'I'm sure we've forgotten something absolutely vital,' said Noel, 'and I've got the most terrible needle.'

'At least you're riding your own pony,' said Alex. 'You haven't got the responsibility of letting down someone else's – which I'm sure to do.'

'From the way you two talk anyone would think you didn't want to enter,' said Christo, putting on her coat. 'And now, if everything's settled, I'm going home. I'm determined to get to bed early.'

'I'm just going to measure the stile, before I go,' said Alex.
'Well, good night, all,' said Henry. 'May tomorrow dawn fair.'
'What a hope,' said Christo.

Chapter 10

THE first action of the members of the Radney Riding Club, when
they wakened on Friday, the first of September, was to leap from
their beds and gaze with sleepy eyes on the weather. Christo, who
rose at six, found a thick silvery haze which obscured the garden
and the sky. It foretold a fine day, she thought, but she cursed as
she ran through the dripping garden, for Dragonfly would be
difficult to find and much too wet to groom.

The shrill voice of David's alarum clock called him punctually
at six-thirty. He didn't usually rise so early on gymkhana morn-
ings, but today was rather important, and he was going to plait
Tanzy. It was a ghost world, he thought, looking out of his window. The trees and shrubs were strange humped figures seen
through the thinning haze and the only sound was a chorus of
drips; trees, walls and roofs dripping monotonously.

His feet left dark prints across the grass and he was squelching
inside his shoes by the time he had caught Tanzy. As he tied
her to the garage door the east became radiant; the haze turned
to spun gold; somewhere a bird started to sing. Tanzy was too
wet to groom, thought David, he had better begin by plaiting.

Alex had been forbidden by Henry to arrive at Radney Manor
before half-past eight and so at twenty minutes past, having
breakfasted, he was wandering through Radney village whistling
cheerfully and imagining a gymkhana at which Trappist turned
out to be lame and he hastened home for Oscar, who, miracul-
ously reformed, won the jumping. Deciding that it was rather
hard on Henry to be done out of his classes, he made Trappist's
lameness due to a stone in the hoof. It came on after Henry had
received a red rosette in the Handy Hunter class, and Finch discovered the presence of the stone just as Alex cantered out of the

ring having made a clear round on Oscar. Someone had come forward from the crowd of spectators and offered Alex a hundred guineas for Oscar. He refused it, explaining that he would never part with his pony. He saw the prospective buyer's disappointed face, he saw himself turn to pat Oscar, who nuzzled him affectionately, and then his dream shattered and suddenly he realized that he had passed the Manor gates and was walking aimlessly in the wrong direction. Looking round guiltily, he turned and ran back at full speed.

The Marlowes had meant to get up very early indeed, but their alarum clock had failed to ring. The haze had disappeared, the dew was drying and the sun was high in the sky when they were wakened by their mother. They wasted precious moments in argument.

'It was your fault, Fanny. You set it,' said Deb angrily.

'Well, you fiddled with it afterwards, you know you did,' answered Fanny. 'I told you to leave it alone, but you wouldn't; I expect you moved the knob.'

'I didn't, I'm perfectly certain I didn't,' yelled Deb. 'You set it wrong.'

'I'm positive I set it properly,' said Fanny. 'You moved it. You're always fiddling with things and trying to lay the blame on me.'

'I'm not.'

'You are.'

'Oh, *do* shut up,' wailed Graham. 'It's half-past eight and we shall never be ready. The ponies will be a disgrace to the riding club and everyone will be *so* cross.'

To make matters worse Swansdown refused to be caught. After twenty minutes of fruitless pursuit Fanny suggested that Deb and Graham, who were rapidly becoming tearful, should begin to groom Golly while she tried by herself. She trailed round after Swansdown crying plaintively, 'Oh, Swansdown, please, please, be caught.' It wasn't until Fanny's despair had given way to resignation that Swansdown gave in and walked straight up to her.

Eric didn't bother to get up early. He told his mother at breakfast that the show would be a very amateurish affair, and that she needn't bother to plait Princess, for there wasn't even a showing class. Mr Lawson said that he would have liked to come along to help out with the organization and see fair play, but work called.

He said that he expected that there would be a good many false verdicts with those kids from West Barsetshire trying to judge. Though he had no time to spare and no wish for the task it seemed ridiculous that, with him at hand, they should send for a pack of kids who knew nothing whatever about judging. In fact, he thought it something of a slight, particularly after all he had done for them, getting Sanderson over and turning up to help at the rally, which was more than any of the other parents could say for themselves.

'Henry's a jolly sight too pleased with himself to listen to suggestions from other people,' complained Eric through a mouthful of sausage. 'He gasses on for hours and hours, and then when anyone else puts a word in he twists it round and gets a cheap laugh from those Marlowe kids. One thing is,' Eric continued, pushing his sausage plate away and starting on toast and marmalade, 'that he'll soon throw the club over when he finds the gymkhana's a flop and he doesn't get anywhere with all this dressage stunt. Then I'll step into his shoes. You can be president, Dad, and Paulina's agreed to be secretary.'

Paulina rose a few minutes earlier than usual because she had decided to plait Starshine's mane.

Personally, she preferred to see a long flowing mane floating artistically on the breeze, but she decided to follow the dictates of fashion. She plaited quickly, fastening the long and ill-assorted lumps with rubber rings. Her grooming took even less time, and she was able to sit down by the rockery and read an historical novel by her favourite author until it was time to bridle Starshine and start for Radney. As she rode along, humming softly, she wondered whether her absence during the preparations of the day before had been noticed. It was a little naughty of her not to have helped, she supposed, but she wasn't one of those strong hefty girls like Christo and surely any complaints would be silenced by the cup – a magnificent silver challenge cup, which her mother was presenting to the club. It was to be awarded to the winner of the senior jumping class and none of the members knew of its existence yet.

To Juliet, half the pleasure of competing in the gymkhana lay in the preparations; in the novelty of early rising; in the before-breakfast sock and tail washing; in the bustle of grooming and, lastly, in the sight of the two ponies. Tomahawk round and red, with his black mane closely hogged, his little hoofs oiled, his tail brushed out and his cheeky eyes shining with excitement; and Romeo a glistening bay with snowy socks and his thin black mane neatly plaited. It didn't matter to Juliet if he were too long in the leg or too light in the neck, to her he seemed the most beautiful pony in the world. She could stand and gaze at him for hours or until her mother called from the landing window that she would be late if she didn't come in to dress.

Henry and Noel began work at half-past seven. They carried out the secretary's table and several chairs. They tightened the ring ropes and filled the buckets of water for the Apple and Bucket race. Then they visited the stables on the way in to breakfast. Trappist had spent the night in, and the two grey heads looked very handsome gazing across the yard at their owners. Sonnet whinnied hopefully; Echo kicked his door when Henry went to speak to Trappist, he wanted some attention.

As they were leaving the stables Alex appeared. 'Good morning,' he said. 'Isn't it a lovely day? It looks like being a scorcher.'

'You sound very cheerful,' said Henry. 'No needle yet, I suppose?'

'Oh, shut up, don't mention it,' said Noel.

'We're just going to have breakfast,' said Henry. 'Oh, by the way, did you remember the barbed wire?'

With a cry of horror, Alex turned and fled down the drive.

After breakfast Henry and Noel opened the gates, pinned up the notice saying Collecting Ring and carried out the rosettes, the prize money and the Thornton Challenge Cup. Christo was bringing the lists of entries over with her, for she had spent the night before drawing the numbers for the various heats out of a hat so that everything should be quite fair.

Mrs Thornton had said that they could borrow Sid to collect the five shillings for the ringside car-park from the cars, and he appeared on the showground at an early hour. Having arranged a chair and table for himself by the gate, he said that half the ring stakes were lopsided and that the rope wasn't tight enough and, fetching the mallet, he started to alter everything. Just as it was time for Henry and Noel to change into their tidy clothes, the secretaries arrived. Angela was wearing a pink cotton dress with brown squiggles, brown shoes and pink-rimmed spectacles. She looked calm and efficient, and Noel could imagine her soothing down an irate employer or dealing with unwelcome visitors. She appeared a perfect private secretary, except that she looked too truthful to tell white lies or invent excuses on the spur of the moment. While Christo put Dragonfly in the loose-box she was borrowing for the day, Henry handed the prize money, the riding-stick, which was the special prize in the under-fourteen jumping class, and the Thornton Challenge Cup over to Angela.

'Mrs Carstairs has given a special prize for Class I,' Angela told them. 'It's the sweetest little tie,' she said, scuffling in tissue paper. She produced a blue tie decorated with foxes' masks. 'For the best performance in Class I by a competitor of ten years or under,' she read out. 'But you're not to tell the little ones; it's to be kept secret,' said Angela.

'It's awfully nice,' said Noel.

'It's very good of Christo's mother to give it,' said Henry. 'But you'll have to lock it up if you don't want Deb to see it. She ferrets anything out. Come on, Noel. We must go. We don't want to keep the judges waiting.'

'Do you think they've changed much since Christmas?' asked Henry, gazing up and down the platform and finding no one who in the least resembled the judges.

'No, they've grown a bit, that's all,' answered Noel. 'Wouldn't it be frightful if we had to meet an unknown judge?' she added. 'Think of having to ask all these people –'

'There they are,' interrupted Henry.

The West Barsetshire people were unmistakably horsy. Susan and John were in riding-clothes, Dick wore corduroy trousers and a hacking-jacket. They carried suitcases and hats, and each one wore a red carnation in his buttonhole.

'Well, they're not in the carriage. I've looked on the seat, under the seat and in the rack and they're not there,' said Dick firmly.

'I can't think what I've done with them. I've searched all my pockets,' said Susan.

'Hallo. What's the matter, have you lost something?' asked Henry.

'Susan's gloves,' said Dick.

'Oh, here they are,' said Susan, giving a sigh of relief as she produced a brand-new pair of string gloves from inside her crash cap. 'Thank goodness for that. Now, I wonder where my ticket is?'

John groaned, and Dick said, 'Try your cap again.'

'Do you think we look all right?' asked Dick as they left the station.

'Do we *have* to wear these things?' asked John, waving his bowler about.

'Mine gives me a headache,' said Susan, 'and John wears his over his eyes and he looks *so* funny. I'm sure I shall giggle in the ring if he wears it.'

'I borrowed this object from Father,' said Dick, putting on a sporting tweed cap at a jaunty angle.

'If you put it on properly you'd look like a point-to-point type,' said Henry. 'But, seriously, I think you're all most suitably attired. They're quite a credit to us, aren't they, Noel?'

' 'Andsome is as 'andsome does,' said Noel. 'I only hope that they're not going to be coffee-housing judges. You know, the sort who are too busy talking about their school days to attend and they always fail to see one jump the first jump.'

'Our school days are too grimly near to be a pleasant subject for conversation,' said Dick.

They piled into the car, Henry going in front beside Sid and the other four in the back.

'How are we supposed to judge this Handy Pony test?' asked John as they drove out of the station-yard.

'However you like,' answered Henry, turning in his seat. 'We've arranged a test for the little dears – most of whom can't ride at all – and I suppose you allot so many marks for each part of the test. Time doesn't count.'

'They have to walk, trot and canter, to halt, to rein-back, to ride up a garden path and lead their ponies over a jump,' said Noel.

'Sounds all right,' said Dick. 'I told you that there was nothing to get rattled about, John.'

'I wasn't rattled,' said John indignantly. 'I only wanted to know.'

Conversation languished. All the West Barsetshire people were feeling nervous, though they wouldn't admit it.

'I've got simply terrible needle,' announced Noel suddenly.

'So have I,' said Susan.

'Nonsense. Judges can't have the needle,' said Henry firmly. 'It's undignified.'

'Well, I have got it *and* it's much worse than when I'm only riding.'

'Oh, gosh, I'll never accept an invitation to judge then,' said Noel. 'I think I should die of the needle if it was much worse than the one I've got now.'

'I say, you haven't forgotten your badges, have you?' asked Henry, turning round and gazing at the judges in horror.

'No, no, of course not,' answered Dick

They produced their badges and, by the time they had pinned them on they were driving through Radney village.

'Strange competitors,' said Noel, gazing at a girl on a pony and a boy on a cob, who were riding past the George and Dragon.

'Welcome to the United Nations,' said Henry as the car turned up the drive.

'I don't get you,' said John.

'He means the flags,' said Noel.

'We've a quarter of an hour to spare,' said Henry, looking at his watch as the car pulled up at the front door. 'Would the judges like to wash or look at the stables?'

The judges wanted to do both, so Henry left Noel in charge of them and ran to the showground to see that everyone was at his post, and that the show was ready to begin.

Noel found trying to control the judges a very arduous task. Every few moments one of them would stop to inspect or admire some object of interest. Dick insisted on examining the suits of armour in the hall. Susan simply had to look at some photographs of horses in the passage and then she stopped again to pat the dogs. John found an antique model cannon and he appeared to intend playing with it for the rest of the day. There was no time for them to see the stables. An exasperated Noel handed them writing-pads and pencils, and hurried them into the ring.

Henry rushed into the ring looking like an American film director; he was coatless and his hair hung over his face.

'The microphone's gone wrong,' he hissed at Noel. 'Go and see if you can persuade the Handy Pony people into the collecting ring.'

Noel found the Marlowes. Deb was tearing about flapping her legs, waving her arm and shrieking at everyone to note the smartness of Golly's newly hogged mane. Graham was dreamily polishing his specs, Fanny was receiving last-minute instruction from Juliet.

'Competitors for Class I into the collecting ring, please,' said Noel.

'I can't go first,' wailed Fanny. 'It's no good, I just can't go first.'

David was standing at the far end of the field. He had Tanzy's reins looped round one arm and he was gazing intently at something which he held in the hollow of his hand. He appeared to have forgotten the existence of the gymkhana.

'David,' shrieked Noel.

'Hallo,' he said, looking up. 'Just look at this – it's the most peculiar-looking chrysalis. I can't think what it can be.'

'For goodness' sake go to the collecting ring,' said Noel. 'We're hours late in starting, and all you do is to collect caterpillars.'

'Oh, O K,' said David, looking at her as though she needed humouring. He wrapped the chrysalis carefully in his handkerchief and placed it in his pocket. Then, very slowly, he mounted and rode towards the collecting ring. Noel waved frantically at Alex, who cantered up to find out what was the matter, and sent him to join the others in the collecting ring.

Suddenly the microphone came to life; it was Bill's voice saying, 'Blast,' which came over the air, followed by a muffled giggle. Gerry stopped adjusting the amplifier and rushed to the microphone. Bill dashed across to the other end of the ring to hear what Gerry sounded like. 'One, two, three, four,' said Gerry, counting over the microphone in a professional manner. Bill waved his arms which meant that he could hear perfectly. Gerry was announcing that Class I was about to begin and that Alex Turner on Trappist would be the first competitor, when Henry returned panting for breath and carrying the megaphone.

'Thank heaven for that,' he said, chucking the megaphone under the secretary's table.

'It sounds quite like a horse show now,' said Juliet.

'Good luck, Alex,' shouted Noel.

Alex rode the Handy Pony test very slowly and solemnly but with great accuracy. Noel thought that he was doing well, but Henry said that if all the competitors took as long the gymkhana would go on until midnight. However, David, who was the second competitor, took only a very short time. He accomplished the walking and trotting successfully, but, in the middle of the cantering, Tanzy suddenly swerved and, taking David by surprise, galloped out of the ring. David's legs shot forward, he leaned back and his hands went up to his chin. Noel remarked in disheartened accents that he might never have had a lesson in his life.

'Out,' shouted the judges.

Gerry, who had not been attending, was caught without another competitor ready to go in. The judges stared hopefully at the collecting ring, Henry fumed.

'What on earth does Gerry think he's doing? Doesn't he realize that we're already behind time?' he demanded.

'The next competitor is number eight, Fanny Marlowe riding Miss Naughton's Romeo,' announced Gerry. 'Now Number 9, you're next,' he told one of the outsiders, 'and Number 1, that's Deborah Marlowe. You're after Number 9, and don't go away whatever you do.'

Fanny rode smoothly and quietly, but her performance wasn't very accurate, and it seemed to take her several yards to stop and start Romeo.

Gerry announced the outsider who followed Fanny as Miss Prue Clarke on Freckles. The Radney Riding Club members eyed her suspiciously, but she didn't look a very formidable adversary. Her arms and legs waved and Freckles was a thickset bay pony, with an untidy mane and tail, who did not wear a noseband. Prue Clarke kicked frantically all the time she was in the ring, but she was quite unable to make Freckles either canter or reinback. Deb and Golly gave a very competent performance until they reached the leading-in-hand jump – the very last part of the test – there Deb absent-mindedly let go of Golly, who trotted briskly back to the collecting ring. Roly, who followed Deb, found it hard to keep Tomahawk under control and he was unable to pull up from the canter in the proper place. Then, when he came towards the leading-in-hand jump Tomahawk suddenly took charge, and before Roly could dismount, he found himself flying over the jump. The audience – quite a few people had arrived by this time – clapped loudly, and Roly, looking very red in the face, galloped into the collecting ring.

The Landon twins – chubby-looking children riding fat grey ponies called Tweedle-dum and Tweedle-dee – both completed the course, but they cantered on the wrong leg and they took ages to mount.

Henry decided that it was time for competitors in Class II to get up.

'Come on, Christo,' he said to her, pausing by the secretary's table.

'All right, in a sec,' said Christo wearily. She and Angela were trying to give out numbers to a queue of competitors, work out how much change they owed a large boy who had just made some late entries, and convince Jeanette Sumner that she couldn't ride two horses in the bareback trotting race.

'I don't really see why I shouldn't,' said Jeanette, who was a pale, sharp-faced girl with lank straw-coloured hair. 'At the Leckhampton Show last week they let everyone ride two horses in all the gymkhana events.'

'Well, this isn't the Leckhampton Show, and we're perfectly entitled to refuse entries,' Henry told her. 'Come on, Christo,' he added. 'Angela will deal with these numbers.'

Paulina rode up to them as they crossed the field. She carried a square cardboard box.

'Pandora's box,' she said gaily. 'But its secret is about to be revealed. May I put it beside the other cup on your table, Christo?'

'Another cup?' asked Christo. 'Oh, whizzo! Yes, of course you can put it on the table. Angela will keep an eye on it.'

'Has your mother presented it?' asked Henry.

'Yes, she thought the seniors deserved a challenge cup, too,' said Paulina. 'It's for the senior jumping.'

'That's perfect,' said Henry. 'Please thank her very much from all of us. We'll write a proper thank-you letter after the gymkhana.'

'The mothers have really been rather good about prizes,' said Noel.

'I expect Eric will win the Swindon Cup,' said Christo.

By the time that Henry, Noel and Christo were back at the ringside Gerry was announcing Herbert Suster on Black Diamond as the last entry in Class I. Herbert was a very small mutton-fisted boy and Black Diamond was nearly fourteen-two. Despite a great deal of hauling and wrenching Herbert seemed unable to stop. He took the garden path at a fast trot and scattered the bars which marked it to the four winds. Black Diamond obviously hadn't been taught to rein-back, and Herbert, who didn't use his legs, tugged at the reins in vain. However, he was much more agile than the Landons and scrambled on in a moment after the leading part of the test.

'Now for us,' said Christo. 'Are you going first, Henry?'

'I hope Alex is going to remember to arrange his wire,' said Henry, looking round anxiously. 'Everything else seems to be ready.'

'Gerry ought to be collecting us,' said Christo

'Will the following numbers go into the ring, please,' announced the microphone and, in response, Alex, Fanny, Graham and one of the strangers rode in. Alex was first and second was Number 8, Hamish Drummond on Keltie. Fanny was third and Graham reserve. Bill rushed in with the rosettes and prizes, and after a slight muddle about which way round the prize-winners should line up, Susan presented them.

'Graham's won your mother's special,' said Henry to Christo. 'Thank heaven it wasn't Deb, or she would have been more unbearable than ever.'

'Jolly good, Alex,' said Noel, clapping loudly as he cantered past.

There was a slight delay before the second class began. The competitors in the Handy Hunter had to congratulate the winners of the Handy Pony, and Alex had to tie Trappist's rosette on his bridle and give him some oats before he could arrange the pretence wire. Henry took in the stop-watch and explained the competition to the judges, and then Gerry sent in the first competitor – Eric on Choc-Bloc. Eric made a clear, but not a very fast round; he fumbled for some time at Alex's wire. Henry on Echo followed. Henry had said that he wasn't going to hurry as it was Echo's first show and he didn't want to upset him, but he wasn't particularly slow until he reached the wire. There, Echo refused to stand still; each time Henry leaned forward to unhook it, Echo backed away. Everyone began to wonder whether Henry would ever manage to do it, and then Echo knocked one of the posts over, and, jumping the debris, Henry rode on and finished the course.

'I don't know whether the jump will ever be the same again,' said Henry to Christo as he rode back into the collecting ring.

'Alex and David are taking long enough over the repairs,' said Christo, who was the next competitor. Dragonfly knocked down

three fences with her forelegs and refused to let Christo touch
the barbed wire. They battled for several minutes and then the
judge called, 'Out, please.' And a shame-faced Christo left the
ring.

In the collecting ring Noel was panicking. 'I'm sure I shan't be
able to undo it,' she told Henry. 'I'm hopeless at knots, and if
you and Christo couldn't undo it I certainly shan't be able to.'

'Nonsense. Don't wail so, you sound just like Fanny,' said
Henry, 'It's perfectly easy if your horse will stand still. I say,
Gerry's shouting his head off; I expect he wants you.'

'Oh, gosh, not already!' said Noel, riding forward hastily.

'If you're Number 27, for Pete's sake go in,' said Gerry in har-
assed accents.

Sonnet also jumped a clear round and she stood perfectly at the
wire but, even so, Noel took rather a long time. She said afterwards that her hands were numb with the needle. Jeanette Sumner, who had been having a practice jump by her horse-box and
making a great deal of noise over it, rode into the ring on her cob,
Lassie, which wore a hood. Jeanette rode with very short stirrups
and seemed to support herself by the reins; she was very quick,
unhooking the wire in a moment, but Lassie hit the second pole
of the in-and-out. Juliet and Paulina made competent, but undis-
tinguished rounds. A boy called Michael Trew on a very stout
cob called Bess and Helen Barbersley on Swift, both had three
refusals at the first fence. Betty Clarke, who was a larger edition
of her sister Prue and also rode Freckles, ran out three times on
the course and was disqualified. Eric, on Princess, galloped round
much faster than anyone else until he came to the wire, and there
he spent very nearly as long as Christo.

Henry on Trappist was the last competitor and he felt very
determined as he rode down to the start, for he knew that if
he didn't do well either Eric or Jeanette Sumner would be the
winner. Trappist went round like a whirlwind. He cleared
every jump with ease and Henry wasted no time over the
wire.

'Jolly good,' shouted Christo as he rode out.

'First-class effort,' said Alex.

'I believe Trappist's going in for red rosettes today,' remarked
Juliet.

'No leaping to conclusions,' said Henry.

But when the results were announced Juliet was right. Henry was first, Eric, on Choc-Bloc, second, Jeanette third and Noel reserve.

'And now for lunch,' said Henry as he cantered out of the ring with Trappist's red rosette in his mouth.

Finch was waiting to take the two greys. 'You go and look after your judges, I'll see to 'er,' he said to Noel, who was loosening Sonnet's girth.

Mrs Thornton had provided an excellent lunch for the judges. Henry had spent the week before telling her all the things she wasn't to give them to eat, for, in spite of having a cook and greenhouses, the Thornton food was inclined to be dull. But now, after devouring cold chicken and vast quantities of an elaborate salad, the judges were presented with dishes of strawberry ice, peaches and cream. Henry dispensed draught cider, and Susan became so giggly that afterwards they made her drink coffee though she said that she hated it, because Henry said that it would sober her up and that he wasn't going to have drunken judges in his ring.

The judges were not allowed to linger over their coffee and they were back in the ring punctually at two o'clock. Unfortunately it had not occurred to any of the riding club members on the showground that the jumps should be arranged at the appropriate heights for Class III, and so Henry and Noel, cursing under their breaths, rushed round frantically, while the judges discussed the rules for judging jumping and drew horses' heads on their writing-pads.

At last everything was ready and Gerry sent in the first competitor: Herbert Suster on Sultan. Sultan was a hot, chestnut, blood pony; he took the first two jumps very fast and then galloped Herbert straight out of the ring.

'Out,' shouted the judges with one accord.

Gerry announced Miss Deborah Marlowe on Golly. Despite Deb's windmill leg aids Golly refused once each at the brush fence, the stile and the wall, and was disqualified. A very downcast Deb returned to the collecting ring. Susan Sinclair, a small pale girl, who wore her hair in pigtails and rode a fat brown pony called Nobby, refused three times at the first jump, and Roly and Tomahawk got as far as the wall before they were disqualified.

Henry, sitting at the ringside with Noel, was beginning to fidget and bite his nails. 'What an appalling standard of riding,' he muttered. 'I don't believe anyone's going to get round.'

'Perhaps we've made the course a bit high,' ventured Noel. 'Not many of the second string have ridden in a show before.'

'A nice exhibition for the spectators,' said Henry savagely. 'Millions of people *would* come to watch just because the second string are in a refusing mood. There,' he added as Herbert Suster and Black Diamond had their third refusal, 'I told you no one was going to get round.'

Noel looked about her. There were about forty cars parked at the ringside, Fanny was riding in on Swansdown.

'Not much hope of her getting round,' said Henry. But, to everyone's surprise and delight, Fanny completed the course with eleven faults: two jumps down and one refusal.

The atmosphere of the gymkhana changed as Alex entered and jumped a clear round in excellent style.

'He's won it,' said Henry.

But the next competitor, Hamish Drummond on Keltie – a dark-brown moorland pony with a mealy nose – also jumped a clear round. Then David rode in and, much to everyone's surprise, he jumped the brush without a refusal. The members' amazement grew as he cleared one jump after another, keeping Tanzy under control by bringing her back into a trot between the fences.

'Another clear round,' said Noel a moment too soon, for Tanzy failed to clear the triple.

'We must go and congratulate him,' said Henry. He and Noel hurried to the collecting ring as Prue Clarke – the last competitor – began her round.

Mrs Rice-Greene was in the collecting ring also congratulating David.

'I couldn't believe my eyes,' she said. 'Mrs Swindon said, "This is your boy, isn't it?" And you were simply sailing round. "It can't be," I told her. "David always comes out at the first jump".'

David was looking red in the face and very embarrassed 'Don't make such a fuss, Mummy,' he said as Henry and Noel came up. 'After all, I didn't do a clear round or anything.'

'You rode her marvellously,' said Noel.

'It was a terrific performance,' said Henry. 'You're third, anyway. Who's reserve, is it Fanny?'

'No, this person who's just finished only had eight faults,' Alex told him.

'Well, good luck for the jump off. Don't let Trappist take the gate too fast, but push him on for the triple.'

'Of course, I tell him it's the riding club he has to thank for it,' Mrs Rice-Greene was saying to Noel. 'I mean, really, he hadn't a clue before it came on the scene, not a clue.'

With the jumps at slightly over three feet Trappist made another clear round. Hamish Drummond and Keltie, who seemed to find them a little high, collected twelve faults. Mrs Thornton, looking very regal, presented the Challenge Cup to Alex and the special prize – a riding-whip – for the best round by a pony under 13.2 to Hamish Drummond. David was third and Prue Clarke reserve.

'Trappist looks like a Communist,' said Henry as he watched his pony canter round the ring with three red rosettes on his bridle.

'He's doing awfully well today,' said Noel.

The senior members of the riding club mounted hastily as Gerry began to call for competitors for Class IV – the jumping competition for riders between fourteen and eighteen years of age. The second string, having handed their ponies to long-suffering parents or tied them to the nearest fence, rushed into the ring and began to adjust the jumps to the appropriate height. Noel and Henry jumped Sonnet and Echo over a practice jump.

Jeanette Sumner told Gerry that she wanted to jump first.

'I'm riding twice,' she told him, 'and I want to get them both round before the jumps get cut up by people refusing. I know what it's like at these one-eyed little shows. I'll jump first and fifth, and that'll give me time to change my saddle.'

Gerry resisted an inclination to tell her that she would jump when she was told, but as she rode into the ring on Fairgame he hoped that she would have three refusals or fall off. Holding Fairgame back – he was strapped down with two martingales – until his canter between his fences was as slow as his walk, Jeanette jumped a clear round. The spectators applauded loudly, but Eric was scowling as he rode into the ring on Princess; he had expected an easy win. Princess jumped a clear round.

Paulina lowered the standard of jumping by running out three times on the course and Helen Barbersley lowered it even more by refusing the first jump three times. Jeanette Sumner, to the club members' dismay, made another clear round; this time she was riding Lassie. And then, to her own surprise and everyone else's delight, Juliet jumped a faultless round. She came out patting Romeo frantically and shrieked to the collecting ring at large that it was the first clear round she had ever jumped in her life. Henry, keeping very calm and riding with great judgment, jumped a clear round on Echo. Betty Clarke on Freckles made four faults and Michael Trew on Bess refused the first jump twice and was disqualified at the second. Then Noel rode in telling herself that Sonnet could jump the course with ease and that it would be her fault if anything went wrong. Eric, awaiting his turn on Choc-Bloc, began to grumble as it became obvious that here was another clear round.

'It's ridiculous,' he said; 'the jumps are far too low. We ought to have begun with them at three feet six, then we'd have weeded out the hopeless people. As it is, every Tom, Dick and Harry is jumping a clear round.'

Christo disagreed. 'We want to encourage the members, not make them have three refusals,' she said. 'It's not as though we've an enormous entry and we can put the jumps up for the jump off.'

There were three more clear rounds. Christo, Henry on Trappist, and Eric on Choc-Bloc made no faults. The judges announced that the nine competitors who had made clear rounds would jump off round the whole course, which had been raised to about three feet nine. To the people who were used to jumping in shows the jumps appeared quite a reasonable size, but to Juliet they seemed enormous. The second string all did their best to encourage her. Deb said that the jumps weren't half as big as they looked, Roly *knew* that Romeo was going to jump them, and Alex said her blood would be up and then one could jump anything. The club members were not at all pleased when Jeanette and Fairgame jumped another clear round; they clapped half-heartedly and assumed sporting smiles to conceal the disappointment which they felt at heart. The disappointment grew as Eric on Princess, Juliet and Henry on Echo all made faults. Not that Juliet was disappointed, she had never expected to win a prize and she was delighted to think that she and Romeo had jumped such an immense course with only eight faults. The second string were becoming noisy.

'Now, come on,' they shrieked at Noel. 'You've simply *got* to do a clear round.'

'You must, you must, you must,' chanted Deb, skipping up and down.

'Oh, do shut up,' said Noel. 'You're making my needle ten times worse. I shall be so flustered I'll ride Sonnet all wrong and she'll hit everything.'

Noel took the first jumps slowly, then she pushed on, cleared the parallels easily, and took the triple faster still.

'Hurray,' shouted Deb, and all the riding club members clapped madly.

'Now, Christo, you're to continue the good work,' Henry told her.

'What a hope,' answered Christo as she rode into the ring. Dragonfly wouldn't come back to hand. She fought for her head as she approached each fence and, in consequence, she brought down both the stile and the gate with her forelegs. The second string groaned loudly as they rushed to put up the jumps. There were still two members of the riding club to jump off; Henry and Eric on their second horses and both of them made clear rounds.

The judges consulted together for a few moments and then announced that the four competitors with clear rounds would jump off over the wall, gate, parallels and triple. The four finalists watched the jumps being raised to what Noel said was an incredible height, and Eric told her, rather scornfully, was a mere four feet. Jeanette shortened her stirrups another hole and took a firmer grip of her plaited reins. Gerry was beginning to enjoy himself; he felt as though he were broadcasting some important sporting function.

'The four competitors who completed the course without faults will now jump off again,' he announced. 'First in the ring is Miss Jeanette Sumner riding Fairgame.'

Fairgame cleared the first three fences with that exaggerated lift of the heels which denotes a horse that has been rapped. The atmosphere in the collecting ring was tense with excitement as Jeanette turned for the triple. The younger members of the second string were willing her to hit the jump, and it was either their will power or the fact that Jeanette held Fairgame back too long – for the triple had been widened as well as raised – that caused him to jump short and crash the top pole.

'Hurray,' said Deb, and was promptly told not to be unsporting by at least seven people.

'Noel, you've simply *got* to beat her,' said Deb not at all abashed.

Alex said, 'Do leave her alone, Deb. You're enough to fluster anyone.'

'I'm going to hit all of them,' said Noel. She patted Sonnet and reminded herself that, whatever happened, she had won a rosette. Sonnet pricked her ears and pulled a little as Noel rode her into the ring. She wanted to get at those jumps again. Noel managed to keep her going steadily for the wall and gate, but Sonnet got away from her as they approached the parallels and took off too far away. Everyone held his breath as he waited for the poles to fall, but, with an extra whisk of her hindquarters, Sonnet cleared them and Noel had her under control again as they turned for the triple. They thundered down the ring and flew over – a magnificent jump in perfect time. The clapping was terrific.

'You've won it,' said Henry as Noel jumped off Sonnet in the collecting ring and began to stuff her with oats.

'Of course I haven't,' answered Noel. 'There's still you and Eric, and you'll both do clear rounds. The jumps are lovely – not a bit high.'

'Sez you,' said Henry, riding in with a grin. But Henry was right. Trappist brought down the gate and Choc-Bloc hit the parallel poles.

'Noel's won! Noel's won!' yelled Deb, causing the people standing near her to put their hands over their ears.

'It looks as though Trappist's got to jump off again,' said Alex. But the three competitors agreed to divide so Mrs Swindon, dignified in purple silk and a black hat, presented the cup to Noel and blue rosettes to Eric, Jeanette and Henry.

As they cantered round the ring Christo led in a swarm of people: six gangs and each one briefed to move a special jump. Then, while the second string took off its coats and mounted its ponies and Gerry started to organize them into heats, she, Juliet and Bill put up the bending poles.

Henry handed Trappist over to Alex. 'I've loosened his girths,' he said, 'and I shouldn't get on him until the very last minute; the poor old fellow's having a fairly energetic time.'

Finch took Sonnet; he said that Noel had better get on with her stewarding, and that he would get Sonnet settled and then come back and help.

The bending race, which was for people under fourteen, didn't take very long as there were only nine competitors and they were run off in three heats. Roly, riding at full speed on Tomahawk, beat Herbert Suster and Graham. Prue Clarke, trotting very sedately, beat Alex and David, who both knocked down posts. Fanny, to everyone's amazement, galloped quite fast and beat Susan Sinclair and Hamish Drummond. But, in the final she knocked down a post, and so Prue Clarke was second to Roly and she was third. As soon as the final of the bending was over Alex and Noel rushed into the ring and began to uproot the posts. The other competitors all took off their saddles and began to practise for the bareback trotting race. Deb fell off twice before she even got into the ring, and Herbert Suster was galloping about the show-ground quite out of control. After shouting over the microphone for some time and finally resorting to threats of disqualification, Gerry at last managed to marshal the competitors in the collecting ring and to divide them into four heats. The first one consisted of Lassie, Bess, Choc-Bloc and Dragonfly, and Christo groaned and grumbled when she discovered that she had three cobs against her.

Bess won the heat easily, for the other horses constantly cantered and then they had to be turned in a circle. Susan Sinclair on Nobby rode against and beat Graham and Hamish. Juliet won the third heat, and the competitors in the last heat cantered, but Henry won, beating Betty Clarke and Roly by a short head. Bess won the final even more easily than she had the first heat. Romeo and Juliet were a bad second, Susan Sinclair a close third and Henry was reserve though he didn't deserve to be, for he had cantered almost the whole way.

When the senior members of the club saw Finch, Noel and Juliet arranging the buckets of water and apples, and the second string taking off their ties and preparing for a cold plunge, they began to feel envious.

'Why didn't we make it under eighteen?' asked Christo. 'I feel just like putting my head in a bucket of water, I'm absolutely boiling.'

'I hope the water's iced,' said Roly.

'Can't I take my shirt off?' asked Graham.

'No,' said Alex and David both at once.

In the first heat Deb on Swansdown raced David and Susan Sinclair. Deb was by far the quickest at removing the apple. In a moment she had scrambled on Swansdown and, turning her round in a way which ill-accorded with the principles of dressage, she was galloping back across the ring.

The second heat consisted of Fanny on Romeo, Alex and Hamish Drummond. Alex reached his bucket before the other two, but he was very slow to dismount, and even slower to capture his apple. Fanny didn't seem to like the idea of getting wet; she was still dithering round the edge of the bucket when Hamish remounted and galloped back. In the next heat Graham raced Herbert Suster, though it was hardly a race. First of all, Golly refused to go faster than her slowest trot and Black Diamond refused to stop anywhere near the buckets; he cantered obstinately round the ring until in despair Herbert dismouted in the middle and led him to the buckets. By this time Graham had his apple and was mounting. In the fourth heat Roly beat Prue Clarke by three lengths.

'Three members of the second string in the final,' remarked Henry as he watched them line up. 'They seem to have practised to good purpose.'

As John Manners started them and the four riders surged forward together, everyone in the collecting ring began to shout, calling out the name of the competitor they favoured. 'Go it, Deb,' 'Come on, Graham,' 'Roly, Roly,' they shouted until it became an indistinguishable roar. David began to shout for Hamish because no one else seemed to be. Deb reached her bucket last, but flinging herself off and grabbing the apple in the same motion, she was the first person to remount and she galloped back across the ring, her eyes full of water and her black hair plastered all over her face. Hamish Drummond passed the winning-post less than a length behind Deb. Several lengths behind him came Graham, with Roly close on his heels. When the dripping competitors had been given their rosettes and Bill's suggestion that a special prize should be given to the wettest one had been ignored, Deb, Noel and Finch began to put up the musical poles.

It was odd, but rather peaceful, thought Noel, to see everyone cantering round to a silence and then across the hot dusty field came the notes of the horn with their vivid reminder of autumn days and wet woods. Henry blew it quite well, she thought, as she watched the waves of competitors converge on the poles.

'Alex is out,' said Deb. 'What a shame.'

'Bad luck,' shouted Henry as Alex rode through the collecting ring.

'I'm sorry to let him down like that,' answered Alex, pulling up and patting Trappist.

'Oh, that's all right. I was hoping you'd come out early,' Henry told him. 'After doing so well, he deserves a rest.'

'I'll take him to the stables now,' said Alex. 'Thank you most awfully for letting me ride him, Henry. I've had the most marvellous day.'

'That's all right, it was a pleasure,' said Henry, 'and I think you did very well on him.' He turned back to the ring. Deb had taken out two posts.

'Canter on, canter on, please,' the judges were shouting at the competitors.

Henry didn't keep them cantering for very long. Once round the ring was quite enough, he thought, for tired ponies. Roly and Herbert Suster were out next, and then Helen Barbersley and Susan Sinclair. To Deb's delight Fanny stayed in till very nearly the end and came out with Eric, the last two competitors before the rosette stage was reached. Christo, Paulina, Juliet and Jeanette remained. 'All girls, how disgraceful,' said Henry.

Juliet was out next, then Paulina. The riding club members watched with tense excitement as Jeanette and Christo cantered round, keeping on opposite sides of the ring. Henry waited until they were both level with the pole and then he blew. Christo turned too quickly. Dragonfly slipped on the dry ground and almost fell; the club members groaned. Jeanette galloped flat out across the ring, reached the pole and failed to stop. By the time she had turned Christo and Dragonfly were there, standing smugly beside the pole.

Everyone clapped and cheered. Bill hurried in with the last lot of rosettes and prizes, and then, suddenly, the show was over.

The judges lost their look of authority, took off their badges and pocketed their notebooks. The competitors gazed regretfully at the empty ring, the trodden grass, and the roughly piled jumps. Another show was over. Sadly they collected their coats and halters. The parents looked at their watches, started up their cars and thought about dinner. Angela began to tidy her papers into an attaché-case.

'Thank heaven that's over,' said Henry.

'Next year,' said Christo, 'we'll make it a much bigger affair.'

'God forbid!' answered Henry. 'Next year the second string can run their own beastly gymkhana.'

'Now, all judges and show officials are to come in to tea,' he continued.

Henry took John Manners, Dick Hayward, Gerry, Bill and Angela in to tea. Noel and Susan Barington-Brown said that they would help Christo settle Dragonfly first.

All the way across the showground people stopped them. 'A grand little "do". Just what's needed to encourage the children,' Mrs Landon told Noel.

'I can't thank you enough for bucking David up so,' said Mrs Rice-Greene to Christo. 'And if you could do with another challenge cup – do let me know.'

Henry had no idea whom the effusive mother who accosted him belonged to, until she said that Susan had been *thrilled*. Then he gathered that it was Mrs Sinclair, and cleverly congratulated her on Nobby's success in the trotting race.

'About six people have asked to join the club,' Christo told Noel and Susan as they helped to cut out Dragonfly's plaits. 'I told them that they must apply in writing, and I would put the matter before the committee.'

Tea, which lasted for an hour and a half, was a very gay meal except for a short wrangle between Henry and Alex when Alex said that the challenge cup in the under-fourteen jumping class had been won by Trappist and therefore belonged to Henry, and Henry said that if Alex thought he wanted filthy cups won by other people on his mantelpiece he was mistaken. When Christo at last brought herself to start for home she discovered that Dragonfly was lying down asleep in her box.

'She's tired,' said Henry. And Susan said:

'She looks so comfortable you can't possibly take her home.'

'Leave her till tomorrow,' said Henry. 'Finch won't mind. Noel and I will give him a hand with the mucking out.'

Christo agreed. 'That's super of you,' she said, and it was arranged that she should ride home on the back of Gerry's bike.

'It's time to clean up for dinner,' Henry told the judges when the last of the show officials had left.

'But we've only just had tea,' objected John.

'I shall burst if I have to eat any more, I know I shall,' said Susan.

Chapter 11

AFTER dinner Noel, Henry and the judges retired to the morning-room and once again they discussed the show. They gradually came to the conclusion that it had been a success, and even Henry began to talk about 'next year,' and the improvements they would make. When at last the topic was exhausted and Susan, John and Dick had related all the latest news from West Barset-shire, they played Henry's records. Then Dick borrowed Eliza-beth's guitar and they invented protest songs and sang them, gig-gling over each other's efforts, until Mrs Thornton appeared and said that *surely* it was time they thought about bed?

Susan was sharing Noel's room and it was a very long time be-fore they fell asleep; even so, Susan wakened at seven and not daring to wake Noel so early, read in bed until eight. Breakfast wasn't until nine, so everyone except Henry, who had failed to appear, visited the stables beforehand. Sonnet and Echo were gaz-ing out across the yard and they looked cheerful as ever, Trap-pist seemed tired, and Finch was in Dragonfly's box.

'Did you know this mare was lame last night?' he asked, when they had wished him good morning.

'Lame?' said Noel. 'No, she seemed all right when Christo put her away. Didn't she?' she asked the others.

'She looked all right to me,' said John.

'I can't say I noticed her particularly,' said Dick.

'I helped put her to bed, ' said Susan, 'and I'm sure she wasn't lame then.'

'Sprained 'er suspensory ligament, that's what she's done,' said Finch in gloomy accents.

'A sprain?' asked Noel, looking at him in horror. 'But that means she'll be lame for ages.'

'Six weeks,' said Finch.

'Well, the holidays are nearly over, that's one thing,' said Susan in comforting tones.

'But the one-day event,' said Noel. 'We shan't have a team. What on earth will Henry say?'

'That's what I was wondering,' said Finch. ' 'E's set 'is 'eart on it – but these things will 'appen.'

As everyone anticipated, Henry was cast into despair by the news. He attacked his bacon and eggs savagely and said that if only that idiot Christo hadn't insisted on having a gymkhana and then entered for everything it would never have happened. Now, they might as well give up bothering about the whole affair, for it was obvious that they didn't stand a chance as individuals – it was only as a team that there had been any hope for them.

John said surely there was someone else and Susan offered to lend Golden Wonder. But she was too small for Christo, and there wasn't really time to begin to school another horse. Henry would only groan, and say, 'Blast everything,' to every suggestion until Mrs Thornton looked up from her enormous pile of letters and remarked that his conversation didn't sound very entertaining for his guests. Henry answered that it was difficult to be entertaining when your life's work lay around you in ruins. Noel, resisting an inclination to quote 'If' to him, got up and said that as she had finished, should she ring up Christo? She didn't relish the task at all, but anything was better than sitting and listening to Henry having an attack of temperament and the West Barsetshire people trying to be helpful.

Besides, she wanted to think. Now that it seemed about to fall through, she realized that she did, after all, want to compete. She thought of the riding club members. Eric's dressage was hopeless and, anyway, there was no fun in riding with people one hated. Paulina was useless. Juliet was amenable, but she would never stay in the arena and though she had jumped well yesterday she couldn't be trusted not to run out. That left only Alex. Would he be good enough? Trappist was an experienced pony. Alex wasn't the sort of person who let one down on the day; he rose to an occasion. Noel pondered as she waited for Christo to answer the telephone.

When she returned to the dining-room the others were also discussing substitutes.

'Christo's not as horrified as I expected,' she told them; 'but she's coming over straight away.'

'Lot of good that'll do,' remarked Henry disagreeably.

'But, honestly, I don't think that Alex would be too bad,' said Dick, returning to the earlier topic of conversation.

Henry didn't answer, he pushed back his chair and led the way out to the stables. Finch was poulticing the injured leg with anti-phlogistine.

'Good-morning,' said Henry. 'This would have to happen now.'

'I reckon it was them musical poles,' said Finch, without looking up.

A little later Christo and Alex appeared. When Christo had visited her horse and discussed ways and means of getting her home with Finch, she said to Henry:

'Well, I never was the star turn at dressage, and you'll have just as much chance – no, more – with Eric in the team.'

'Eric?' said Henry. 'But we haven't the least intention of having Eric in the team. He's no idea of dressage and he won't even begin to learn.'

'But he'll get millions of bonus marks for his cross-country,' objected Christo, 'and I'm positive his dressage is no worse than mine.'

'And I'm positive that he won't be in the team at all,' Henry told her. 'If you really want to know we've decided to ask Alex.'

'Alex?' repeated Christo in a voice which expressed amazement. 'But . . .' She stopped abruptly as she realized that he was beside her. Alex was scarlet in the face.

'Me in the team?' he said. 'But I can't jump high enough. I shall let you both down. I'd never won a prize until yesterday and then it was only in miserable under-fourteen classes.'

'Well, we're going to try you out anyway,' Henry told him. 'The curse of it is that Trappist must have a day off today.'

'We could try him on Sonnet,' suggested Noel. And in the end, when they had overruled Alex, who said that he would unschool her, that was what they did.

John and Dick marked out the arena while Alex and Henry saddled their horses and the three girls began to clear up the ring.

Henry produced a very crumpled and decayed-looking copy of the test from his pocket; only to hear that Alex already knew it.

'I've been practising it on Oscar,' he explained. 'I thought dressage might be his metier.'

'Oh, good,' said Henry.

'And was it?' Noel asked.

'No, I don't think so,' said Alex sadly. 'He doesn't seem to enjoy work of any description, but he's much fatter and miles more agreeable,' he added, his face brightening a little.

To everyone's delight, and Christo's intense surprise, Alex rode the test quite reasonably. At least, he remained in the arena and managed to walk, trot and canter at more or less the appropriate spots. To Noel and Henry, his rein-back and turns on the forehand looked very good and his circles and extended trots seemed his worst points. Henry let John and Dick each try Echo, and then he rode the test himself. Noel said that his effort was the best she had seen him do, but that Echo's trot was still too fast and not very balanced. Finally, Noel rode the test on Sonnet and tried to discover whether the others thought she was using her seat more, and if Sonnet's transitions from faster to slower paces had improved, but none of them felt sure enough of themselves to venture a criticism, and Susan would only make flattering remarks.

After lunch – at which the Radney Manor catering suffered a relapse and provided cold sausages, aged lettuce leaves and pink blanc-mange – the West Barsetshire people had to catch their train. Henry and Noel accompanied them to the station and saw them off, acknowledging their cries of 'Good luck on Saturday,' with sickly grins.

Never did six days pass so quickly as those between the riding club gymkhana and the Letchdale Dressage Group's Horse Trial. The Radney Riding Club received a communication saying that the dressage time of their members would be 11.00 a.m., 11.08 and 11.16, which drove them to further frantic efforts at self-improvement. Henry was in an almost permanent state of collapse through so much riding without stirrups and Noel began to hate the sight of trees as she rode round and round with her eyes fixed on them rather than on the ground. With Alex they were careful not to demand too much and they tried to be as encouraging as possible. The cross-country was his worst point. He was so cautious, always slowing Trappist up for corners, and he seemed incapable of galloping really fast downhill.

'We don't want you to be wild,' Henry told him, 'but at the pace you're going at the moment you'll collect penalty marks. You must try and push on a bit.'

Alex tried, but he simply didn't seem able to go any faster.

'Look, why not put Christo on Trappist?' he suggested. 'I'm obviously going to let you down.'

But Henry said that Christo was much too heavy for a fourteen-two pony and that if anyone let down the team it would be him.

On Thursday Echo's trot was worse than ever and Henry, unable to decide whether it was Echo's back that had gone stiff or his own legs that had gone weak, bumped round and round the school and became sunk in despair.

'He won't stride out properly however much I use my legs,' he complained to Noel. 'I wish I'd never heard of this wretched competition. I'm obviously going to muck up everything.'

Noel tried to be helpful and consoling, but it was no use. Henry, looking hotter and more cross with each moment, schooled feverishly in a disagreeable silence.

But on Friday the fruits of Thursday's schooling appeared. Echo was using his hocks much more than usual. Henry's spirits rose.

'In future my motto's going to be "Say not the struggle naught availeth",' he told Noel.

'You'd better write it in all the second string's autograph books,' said Noel. 'Deb wanted me to write a horsy quotation in hers, but I refused. I wrote, 'I strove with none for none were worth my strife." I thought it might be good for her character.'

'I think Alex had better stop riding now,' Henry continued. 'Trappist goes much better if he's fairly fresh and he's done just over half an hour.'

'Supposing we take Sonnet and Echo out for a short hack?' suggested Noel. 'We don't want them to be too stale for to-morrow.'

So Sonnet and Echo went for a quiet ride round the lanes, and Henry, who hadn't hacked Echo for some time, was pleasantly surprised by the improvements in his manners and balance.

'This is marvellous,' he told Noel. 'I can ride him in one hand and he's given up shying.'

It was about a sixty-mile drive to Cadlington in Letchdale,

where the horse trial was being held. By six o'clock on Saturday morning Finch, Henry and Noel were all at work, and at six-thirty Alex joined them. The riders were grooming and Finch was putting up the manes. Trappist and Sonnet had both managed to stay clean, and they looked marvellous when they were led into the box. Sonnet went first, walking briskly up the ramp with pricked ears, Trappist followed her and Echo gave a couple of snorts and then walked up with no trouble at all.

'Now 'ave you got everything? 'Aynets, buckets, sack of feed. Tack, that's all there, grooming kit. Now, 'ave you got your 'ats and sticks?'

'Yes, and gloves. But we're not going to wear them if it's as hot as this,' answered Henry.

'Well, good luck,' said Finch. 'And mind you bring back some ribbons.'

'Thanks awfully, Finchey,' said Henry. 'I wish you were coming. Next stop Waylebury,' he added, as he climbed into the box and banged the door, for that was where they were picking up Christo. They waved to Finch as they drove away down the drive, but Henry's attention was soon claimed by Echo, who, frightened by the branches of the trees scraping the roof of the horse-box, began to jump about and kick. Henry calmed him. Alex sat down on a haynet and said that he was going to sleep. Noel admired Sonnet's appearance and wished that she could plait as well as Finch, then she sat down on one of the seats and was half-asleep by the time they reached the Wellington Arms, where Christo was waiting.

'You do look a lively party,' said Christo sarcastically as she boarded the box.

'Shush, we're conserving our strength,' Henry told her.

As the day grew older and the sun rose higher, the horse-box became hot and stuffy. Everyone took off his coat.

Henry said that it was time for elevenses and, opening the picnic basket, he handed round coffee and biscuits. 'A quarter to ten,' he said when they'd eaten. 'We ought to be nearly there.'

'What's the name of the place?' asked Christo.

'Fernley Park, Cadlington, Letchdale,' answered Henry.

'I believe we're lost,' said Christo a moment later as the horse-box pulled up. 'He's asking the way.'

'Oh, heaven help us,' said Henry. They drove on again and

then, at the next crossroads, they turned, with a great deal of reversing, and drove back the way they had just come.

'Oh, curse,' said Henry.

Their anxiety grew as the minutes passed and they still didn't arrive.

'Ten-fifteen, and I can't even see a notice saying to the Horse Trials,' said Christo.

'We shan't have much time for riding round and loosening the horses up,' said Henry, who was biting his nails. A few moments later the box stopped again. This time the driver got out and hurried into a village shop.

'Do you think he's asking his way or buying cigarettes?' demanded Henry angrily.

'Asking the way,' said Noel, who was wondering if she would be glad not to enter after all.

'We shall never get there at this rate,' said Henry, when the driver failed to reappear.

'You're certainly going to be late. I hope they won't disqualify you all if you're not there by eleven,' said Christo.

'Where on earth has he got to?' asked Henry, getting out of the box and looking round. The driver appeared.

'There's some queer folks in these parts,' he said. 'They're all either deaf or daft, or a bit of both.'

'Are we anywhere near Fernley Park?' asked Henry.

'They say it's the other side of Marford — that's the town we just came through,' said the driver in placating tones. 'We're to drive back and then ask again.'

'Oh, lord,' said Henry, getting back into the box.

'It's another hour's journey,' he told the others as the box moved off. 'We may as well give up all hope of competing.'

'I shall go mad in a minute,' said Noel, finding their predicament and Henry's conversation exasperating.

'What about putting the tack on?' suggested Christo. 'Then at least you'll be ready when we do get there.'

'If we ever do,' said Henry.

The riders squeezed in with their horses, and Christo passed the saddles to them. The tack was soon on and still they had not arrived. Henry sighed and kicked the haynets. Noel sat in a corner and resigned herself to the worst. Christo was still hanging out of the window and Alex was telling himself a story of the day.

He was hurtling round the cross-country course at a tremendous speed; clearing solid walls and grave-like ditches with consummate ease. As the horse-box bumped through a gateway and Christo shouted, 'We seem to be arriving,' he and Trappist soared over the water.

'We shall be too late,' said Henry gloomily. 'These affairs are run absolutely dead on time. It's after eleven, so I've no doubt we're disqualified.'

'Well, will you go and find out, while we unbox the horses?' asked Christo.

'You'd better wait until I've found out,' said Henry, jumping down as the box pulled up beside another. 'There's no point in getting them out if we've got to turn round and go home.'

When he had gone Christo said, 'Come on, we may as well get them out, whatever Henry says; they may want you in a hurry.'

By the time Noel and Alex were in the saddle and Christo had tightened Echo's girths and pulled down his stirrups they could see Henry running back across the park. As he drew near they could see that he was smiling, and he waved some numbers over his head.

'Oh, good, it's O K,' said Noel, and the needle attacked her viciously.

'Gosh! I feel sick,' said Alex.

'You look a bit green,' observed Christo.

'It was the horse-box, I expect,' said Noel hastily. 'You'll be all right now you're out in the fresh air.'

'Everything's O K,' said Henry rather breathlessly. 'Their own B team was here so it went instead of us. We're going at their time – 12.45. I've got our numbers. The dressage arena's frightfully grand and there's some frightfully superior horses and dozens of people in black coats. We haven't the ghost of a chance of winning anything.'

The horse-box driver asked if they wanted to put the horses in again, but Henry, remembering General de Veriac's instructions, said no thank you, they were going to ride round and supple them up.

The horses were all very excited, but when Trappist discovered there were no hounds he decided that it was just another dull old show and lost interest. Sonnet gazed at all the handsome horses and watching people, then she arched her neck and lengthened her stride and hoped that they were admiring her. Echo's eyes bulged in the most unsophisticated manner as he gazed about him in amazement, but, though he gave a couple of light-hearted bucks, he remained controllable.

The dressage arena, which, as Henry had said, was a very superior one, was surrounded by a white fence. The markers, looking like one-legged lumps of sugar, stood outside it, and the whole affair was roped off so that the spectators and horses could not get near enough to disturb the horse which was doing the test. The Radney Riding Club team looked critically at the fat man in a black hunting coat who was riding the test on a well-bred chestnut horse.

'He doesn't look very good,' said Henry in a surprised voice.

'The horse seems frightened of his mouth,' observed Noel.

'He's practically star-gazing,' said Henry; 'and the chap on top looks like Eric will by the time he's forty. Perhaps the General was right, and we shan't be the worst after all.'

'The General didn't see me,' said Alex gloomily.

'Oh, you'll be all right,' Henry told him. 'I'm the unpredictable one.'

'Everyone's probably much worse once they're inside the arena,' said Noel.

'Well, I'm going to school Echo over there in the shade,' Henry told the others. 'Trappist doesn't need much exercise, so you can watch for a bit, if you like, Alex.'

Noel said that she must school too, so they left Alex and Christo to watch together.

It was pleasantly cool riding in the dense shade of the big trees; the grass was long and there was a smell of damp earth instead of the cloud of sunbaked dust in which one rode at Radney. Noel, deciding that Sonnet was suppled up, had dismounted and was watching Henry and Echo when Christo came across the park.

'It was frightfully funny just now,' she said. 'A very smart-looking man in scarlet jumped right out of the arena when he was meant to be turning on the forehand.'

'Gosh!' said Noel. 'I hope I don't do that – it would be terribly embarrassing.'

'Look,' said Christo, as Henry rode up, 'I've got a programme and you've hardly any time between the dressage and the cross-country sections. Everyone says you simply have to walk the course, so Alex is putting Trappist in the box, and I thought I could hold Echo and Sonnet while you walked round.'

'Lord, yes. We'd better get a move on,' said Henry, dismounting hastily. 'I'm hopeless; I'd entirely forgotten about the cross-country.'

Though none of the jumps was higher than the promised three feet six, none was lower and all were solidly built. Most of them had guard rails or ditches in front of them and few of them were placed on the level.

The first jump, a long, broad, brush fence sloping away from the take-off, was in the park and the second one, a flight of stout rails, had been built into the fence which separated the park from the adjoining fields.

Below the park the fields sloped steeply and in the valley the pale stubble lay like a golden river. It was hot and dusty trudging up the valley with the sun directly overhead. Noel, feeling very pessimistic, said that the jumps looked huge and she was sure they were over three feet six. Alex looked at the ditches and each moment he became more silent and slightly greener. Three jumps had been built in the stubble field, two double-oxers and a stout grey stone wall. Flags marked the turn which led uphill to the stile and there they found themselves on grass again. Another turn and they approached what they decided was the worst jump of all, a brush fence with a ditch, which Henry said was at least six feet wide, on the take-off side. Alex christened it the grave. Lower down the hill was the drop fence, and almost at right angles to it stood the in-and-out. There were only two more fences, the gate and another flight of rails which led back to the park. Realizing that his companions were filled with gloomy forebodings, Henry did his best to be bracing.

'It's a bad policy to see jumps for the first time on one's feet,' he said. 'It makes them look much worse than they actually are.'

He thought of advising Alex to steady Trappist as he came downhill for the drop fence and turned for the in-and-out, but, remembering his usual cautious pace, he refrained.

He contented himself by saying, 'We shall be all right; they're not half as stiff as they look,' in unconvincing tones.

Back at the horse-box the team put on their coats and hard hats, and Christo tied on their numbers.

'Do you want any lunch?' she asked.

None of them wanted anything to eat, but they all drank orange squash.

Conversation became spasmodic. 'It's stifling in a coat,' said Henry. And Noel asked: 'Who's got the copy of the test? I believe I've forgotten it.'

'Don't be idiotic, you can't have,' said Henry, producing the tattered piece of paper from his pocket.

'Are you sure that you know it?' Christo asked Alex. Alex said that he was.

'We'd better ride in the direction of the collecting ring,' said Henry in a regretful voice.

They arranged with the collecting steward that Henry should ride first, Noel next and Alex last, and then they schooled their horses while the last of the Flintshire people rode the test. Christo was polishing Echo's bit when the collecting steward announced:

'The Radney Riding Club, first member of the team is Number 13, Henry Thornton riding Echo.'

'Good luck,' said Noel, Alex and Christo.

As it was a novice test the judges were allowing the competitors to ride round the arena before the test began. Echo seemed rather apprehensive; he peered nervously at the markers. Henry was using his legs and seat to drive him into his bridle. The senior judge, who sat in the middle of the table, which stood on the raised platform behind 'C,' rang a bell – the signal for Henry to start. Henry turned at 'A' and rode up the centre line.

'He looks quite straight,' said Christo.

'You can't tell from this angle,' said Noel. 'He's walking too quickly.'

'Well, he's halted straight,' said Christo, as Henry took off his hat. 'He looks beyond "X" to me,' said Noel.

'He's keeping round the sides of the arena,' said Alex, 'which is more than some of the people did this morning.'

Henry had forgotten the heat and their chances of winning; he had forgotten his fears that Alex would make a mess of the cross-country section. His mind was empty of everything except Echo – Echo and the movements they were to carry out together. Their extended trots were not good – they lacked impulsion, but their turns on the forehand were excellent. The loose-rein walk was a little hurried; the rein-back a trifle crooked.

'Now for the canter,' said Christo as Henry passed 'B' and began his sitting trot.

'I bet Echo bucks,' said Noel gloomily. Echo didn't buck, but his lead off wasn't particularly smooth and he lost his cadence for a few strides when he began to circle. His canter on the other leg was a little worse; he swished his tail as he led off and he was never quite into his bridle.

'Still, he didn't buck or change legs,' said Noel when the cantering was over and Henry was walking on a loose rein. 'In fact he's done much better than I expected.' She began to ride Sonnet round the collecting ring, remembering that her turn was next.

'Good luck,' said Henry as he rode out and she rode in. He was smiling now that his ordeal was over.

'I shall be miles worse than you,' said Noel.

Sonnet didn't mind the arena. She pricked her ears and gazed about her with calm interest. Noel felt like panicking; she knew that she had gone stiff all over and her legs seemed to have turned to lead. The senior judge rang the bell. At 'A' one turned and rode up the centre line.

'She's weaving about a bit,' remarked Henry in the collecting ring.

'She's halted crooked,' said Christo.

'Noel always begins badly,' observed Henry; 'but usually she calms down after the first moment or two.'

And, as usual, Noel did. Her extended trots felt quite reasonable, she knew that her turns on the forehand were good. It wasn't long before she was cantering. 'A little slower,' she kept telling herself. She rode harder as she turned into the circle, she must try to keep her cadence. She changed the rein at the ordinary trot; she cantered and circled with the near fore leading, she came back to a trot. Transitions were still her weak point, thought Henry.

'Alex,' he said, 'you'd better ride round; keep Trappist moving. She's nearly finished.'

Alex looked more miserable than ever.

'You'll be OK,' Henry told him. 'It's not nearly so bad once you get going, and no one is expecting you to win.'

Noel was bowing to the judges; she was coming out, riding on a loose rein.

'Are you ready?' asked the collecting steward. Alex's moment had arrived, he didn't answer; feeling sicker than ever, he rode in.

Noel jumped off Sonnet and began to stuff her with oats.

'You were first class,' said Henry.

Noel said, 'Our entrance was terrible.'

'I hope Alex isn't going to ride the test with Trappist drooping like that,' said Henry. 'Legs, legs,' he muttered.

The bell rang and Alex turned up the centre. Trappist still had no impulsion, but he was fairly straight. Alex remembered to take off his hat. When he began to trot Alex began to ride and Henry sighed with relief.

'Turns on the forehand seem to be our strong point,' said Henry as he watched Alex ride his second turn.

'He's going well,' said Christo.

'It's a good thing there isn't a time limit,' said Henry. 'He's fearfully slow and solemn.'

Noel thought, it's idiotic to have the needle for Alex as well as myself. Oh, gosh! I do feel awful.

'I hope he's not going to jump out or anything when he starts to canter,' said Henry.

'It's the circles I'm worried about,' said Noel. But, though Trappist led off a little late, Alex managed the cantering very successfully.

'You must admit he's streets better than Eric,' said Henry to Christo.

'For this, yes,' said Christo. 'But I'm not so sure about the cross-country and show jumping.'

'Now you've started my needle off again,' complained Noel.

'Give him his head,' muttered Henry as Alex began his loose-rein walk. Remembering to turn before he reached 'A,' in order to be on the centre line, Alex rode up to 'X' and halted; very slowly he took off his hat.

'You were brilliant,' Henry told him as he came out.

'*Miles* better than I expected,' added Noel.

'It was quite true what you said about being all right once you started,' said Alex, patting Trappist.

Noel produced a handful of oats.

'Now for our practice jump,' said Henry. 'Christo and the driver are going to hold it for us. Come on, everyone. I've got to be at the start of the cross-country in about two minutes.'

Henry had first jump and then, seeing that everyone else was riding in shirt sleeves, he took off his coat and tied on his number again.

'See that they tighten their girths, Christo,' he shouted as he rode away.

When Noel and Alex had taken off their coats and each jumped the practice pole a couple of times they thanked the driver and Christo, who said that she was going to stand between the open ditch and the drop fence; most of the grief seemed to be there.

The starter was relieved to see Noel and Alex.

'Oh, there you are,' he said. 'I was beginning to think that you were lost. Your first man started in fine style. You're a very young riding club, aren't you?' he asked, looking Noel and Alex up and down.

'Yes, I suppose we are,' answered Noel. 'Henry Thornton, whom you've just started, is our oldest member. But I'm only a temporary member as I'm staying at Radney for these holidays; at home I belong to the West Barsetshire Pony Club.'

'West Barsetshire, that's George Holbrooke's pack,' said the starter.

'Yes, that's right,' said Noel.

'He's here today. He's one of the judges for this section. Stationed up on the hill somewhere, I believe.'

'He's supposed to be in France,' said Noel indignantly.

'Here, it's time you were off, young lady. Here I am coffee-housing, and you should be on your way. Get set. Ready? Go!'

Noel had no time to think about the needle; she was over the first two fences and galloping down the hill before she thought at all, and then she remembered Henry's words on bonus marks and gave Sonnet her head. Red flags to the right, she told herself, as she swept round the one at the bottom of the hill. Now she was galloping on stubble, taking the oxers fast, collecting Sonnet a little for the grey stone wall. Sonnet began to puff as she climbed the hill; Noel steadied her for the stile. They were back on grass now, but the open ditch was drawing alarmingly near. Ride at it as though it's a triple, Noel told herself. She increased her speed and Sonnet jumped without hesitation. Steady for the drop fence, she thought, and safely over, slower still for the sharp turn which brought one to the in-and-out. Sonnet hit the second rail of the in-and-out; she hit it hard, but the jumps were fixed so it didn't fall, but it caused her to falter in her stride. Sensing that she was tired, Noel slowed up to give her a breather before the gate, but, even so, Sonnet hit it and almost fell, unseating Noel slightly. However, they cleared the last fence and Sonnet responded valiantly to Noel's call for a last spurt to cover the hundred-yard gallop home.

Henry was waiting at the finishing post. 'Hurray, you made it,' he said. 'Any refusals?'

'No, not one,' said Noel, dismounting and loosening Sonnet's girth. 'Have you any oats?'

'A pocketful,' he answered; 'but I'd let her get her breath first. Me 'eart was in me mouth when you hit the gate, I thought you were down.'

'We hit the in-and-out, too,' said Noel; 'but she jumped the grave marvellously. How did you do?'

'Two refusals, I'm afraid,' answered Henry. 'He didn't like the look of the stone wall or the open ditch – he insisted on a thorough inspection before he went over. We hit the in-and-out too, but it didn't bust, so that's all right. Still, I don't think we lost much time by refusing because he went a terrific speed the whole way and we didn't waste an inch at the turns.'

'I think he was good for a young horse,' said Noel, patting Echo. 'Has Alex started yet?' she asked.

'Yes, he started a moment before you came in,' Henry told her. 'I saw him over the first jump, but that and the last two are all one can see from here. You have to abandon your horse and go right out in the fields where Christo is if you want to see any more. He'll be here any second now, if he hasn't been chucked out for refusing.'

Alex had started slowly and then, as he cleared the second fence, he felt his courage rise and he realized that he had ceased to care for holes or corners or not being able to stop. Suddenly he cared for nothing but the ecstasy of speed – for speed and the music of the wind in his ears as he hurtled down the hill.

The jumps were nothing to him; he rode at them wildly, but Trappist was experienced enough to ignore his rider. He liked to take his fences fast and to choose his own take-off – he preferred the reckless Alex to the overcautious one, who always gave him his head too late.

When Alex saw the long, steep, uphill climb, he did slow up a little and he remembered to ride well forward. The stile was safely negotiated and ahead lay the grave. Alex just had time to realize that he wasn't in the least nervous, and then he was over and it was already too late to steady for the drop-fence. He took it much too fast. Trappist pecked badly on landing, and Alex lost both stirrups and lay on his neck. I mustn't fall – it's sixty points – he thought, and he hung on to the mane and Trappist recovered his balance. Alex turned him for the in-and-out and struggled back into the saddle. He had no time to regain his stirrups so he took a firm hold of the mane and rode at the jump. He stayed on somehow and he was able to get them back in time for the gate, which Trappist cleared by the smallest possible margin. They hit the last fence, but not very hard and then Alex rode all out for the gallop home; he didn't pull up until he was a long way past the finishing post. Noel and Henry were beside him in a moment, asking questions to which he was too breathless to reply. He dismounted and leaned against Trappist as he patted him. Noel loosened Trappist's girths.

'It was wonderful,' said Alex at last. 'It was super and fantastic, and fabulous and everything else at once.'

'Did you refuse anything?' asked Henry.

'No, of course not,' answered Alex indignantly. 'But I nearly fell off. Trappist was wonderful; I've never been so fast in my life.'

'You finished at a pretty good lick,' said Henry.

'Here's Christo,' said Noel, and the boys turned to see her running towards them across the park.

'Well done, all of you,' she said. 'Alex, you were absolutely stupendous but, gosh, I thought you were off at the drop-fence. He jumped the in-and-out without stirrups,' she told Noel and Henry. 'And, honestly, he went a *terrific* pace.'

'I did a shocking turn for the in-and-out,' said Alex. 'I was hanging on to the mane for grim death.'

'I know. I can't imagine how you got round at all,' said Christo. 'I thought, He's had it. Sonnet did the most marvellous jump over the open ditch,' she continued excitedly, 'and, considering Echo's a young horse and everything, you've done heaps better than I expected; honestly, you have.'

Everyone related his feelings over the different fences for

some time, and then Henry said that he thought they ought to walk the horses round for a bit – Trappist was still sweating – before they watered and fed them. Alex announced that he was starving.

When the horses were eating their feeds and the riders, lying on the grass by the horse-box, had started their lunch, Noel suddenly remembered her conversation with the starter.

'Henry,' she said, 'did you know your Uncle G. was judging?'

'What?' asked Henry, pausing in the middle of a mouthful of hard-boiled egg. 'Nonsense, he's in France.'

'The starter said he was a cross-country judge, didn't he, Alex?' Alex agreed.

'Where's the programme?' demanded Henry.

Christo flung it at him.

'You're right,' he said, hastily scanning the front page. 'Well, I don't think we've disgraced him, do you, Noel?'

'Of course you haven't,' answered Christo before Noel had time to reply. 'You've done jolly well.'

'But the West Barsetshire standards are quite different from the Radney and district ones,' explained Henry. 'Don't forget that you all admire Eric, but my Uncle G. would be ill for months if he saw him trying to ride a dressage test.'

'Slight exaggeration,' said Noel; 'but he'd certainly curse.'

'Well, he curses enough at the WB people,' said Henry, 'and none of them are as blatantly bad as Eric.'

'He can't have seen our dressage, anyway,' said Noel.

'I'll tell you who did see our dressage, though – the General,' said Alex. 'I'm sure it was him, he looked at me most intently when I was walking round the arena.'

This information brought fresh cries of horror from Henry and Noel. 'The General will tell Uncle G. Still, if we're bad enough perhaps he'll invite us to Folly Court for a dressage course, and we'll take Alex with us,' said Henry.

'And me,' said Christo.

'Not unless you believe in dressage,' said Henry. 'We shall make you swear the oath of the dressage maniac before we allow you inside the hallowed portals of Folly Court.'

Alex said, 'What is the oath of the dressage maniac?' Henry said that he didn't know; he would invent it on the way home.

When they had finished lunch, Christo, Noel and Alex walked

over to the cross-country course to watch the last few people going round. Henry lay in the shade and refused to move. When the cross-country section was over there was an interval of three-quarters of an hour before the show jumping began. Henry was still lying in the shade when the others returned to the horse-box; Noel and Alex threw themselves down near by. Christo was filled with energy; she polished up the tack and insisted on grooming all the horses, though the riders assured her that they were going to do it in a minute. Then she began to bother Henry.

'I'm sure you ought to go and say hallo to your uncle,' she said. 'It's only polite. Besides, he might tell us how you stand in the marking.'

'Don't be silly, no uncle ever wants to see his nephew,' Henry told her. 'I should only get a preliminary lecture on Echo's lack of balance. Besides, he's probably busy drinking champagne in a luxurious marquee with all the other judges.'

'Well, I think you're feeble,' Christo told him. 'Anyone would suppose you didn't want to know if the team was in the running.'

'I know we're not without asking,' Henry told her.

When the Radney team mounted and rode across to the jumping ring they were all very cheerful, but as they waited in the collecting ring surrounded by the bevy of handsome horses carrying black and scarlet-coated riders, they began to feel small, young and foolishly optimistic.

The course consisted of ten fences arranged in a figure of eight with the last three jumps in the centre of the ring. The jumps were solid looking and the course, with its turns and mixture of straight and spread fences, was one that needed a handy horse.

Everyone who had entered for the competition was allowed to ride in the jumping section even if they had been disqualified during the dressage or cross-country parts of the test, but there were only twenty riders instead of the original twenty-one, as one of the horses had gone lame.

The teams jumped in the same order as they had ridden in the dressage competition. First was the Letchdale 'A' team; three men smartly dressed in scarlet – two of them jumped clear rounds, but the last one knocked down two fences which cost him twenty points. The second team, which was Letchdale 'B,' lost an aggregate of sixty points, and the third team was the one from which the rider had had to retire because of his horse going lame; the two remaining members were only able to compete for the individual prizes, and they lost ten points each.

'Of course the horses are tired,' said Henry. 'Otherwise, I don't believe many of them would hit these jumps.'

'Sonnet doesn't feel tired now,' said Noel. And Christo asked:

'Do you want another practice jump? You're after this Flintshire team.'

'Oh, lord, so we are,' said Henry. 'Yes, I think we do want a practice jump, the horses are probably a bit stiff. Come on, everyone.'

When they had had their jumps they rode back to the collecting ring and found all the spectators clapping. They guessed that someone had made a faultless round. The last member of the Flintshire team rode in and jumped everything clear.

'They're good,' said Christo.

'I'm afraid we shan't do that,' Henry told her. 'I've got an unpleasant feeling that I'm going to add to my sixty lost marks and everyone else's efforts will have been in vain.'

'Don't be temperamental,' Noel told him. 'We agreed ages ago that there was to be no fuss about letting each other down.'

'Number 13,' said the collecting steward, who had just announced the Radney Riding Club.

Henry rode in. Echo, who was becoming used to constantly changing surroundings, looked round the ring in a calm and experienced manner. Henry circled quietly until the judges gave him the signal to start; then, remembering Echo's tendency to refuse the first jump, rode hard at the brush fence. He increased his speed for the parallels and slowed down a fraction for the gate. There was a sharp left turn for the stile; Echo put in a short stride and the top pole fell behind him. The next jump was the wall, and Henry thought of the wall in the cross-country course and, again, he rode hard. Echo faltered, took off too near, but still managed to clear it. Riding diagonally across the ring, Henry jumped the 'Road Closed' and the triple; he turned right and down the centre of the ring stood the oxer, the double gates and a small wall with rails on top. Echo, finding his head turned for home, took off carelessly and hit the take-off rail of the double oxer really hard. Henry collected him for the gates; this time Echo was taking no chances, he lowered his head, chose his take-off and cleared them both easily. The last jump was nothing to him.

'The last competitor lost twenty points,' announced the microphone.

'Oh, dear, I'm next,' said Noel.

'Go on, good luck,' said Christo.

As Noel and Sonnet took each fence, Henry, Christo and Alex held their breath, waiting for it to fall; but fence after fence still stood, and they were becoming jubilant as they watched Noel turn up the centre of the ring. Whether Sonnet's attention was on the second gate or whether Noel held her back a moment too long they didn't know, but both gates fell and they had lost another twenty points.

Alex was fairly calm. 'Leave Trappist alone as much as possible,' Henry told him; 'but don't let him come too fast at those beastly gates.'

'OK, I'll do my best,' said Alex.

Noel, coming out of the ring, said, 'Sorry, everyone.'

'Now who's making a fuss?' asked Henry. 'And, anyway, you had the same number of faults as me.'

'Come on, Trappist, do your stuff,' muttered Christo.

Trappist cleared the first three fences and hit the stile.

'Typical,' said Henry. 'He's always careless over stiles.'

'Oh, dear,' said Noel, as the 'Road Closed' fell behind him.

'Well *done*,' said Henry as Trappist flew over the oxer. 'Careful now,' he added, as he watched him approach the double gates. Trappist knew what he was doing and, with a whisk of his quarters, he cleared each gate in turn.

'Hurray,' said Henry, and then, 'Oh, curse,' for the top rail of the wall had fallen.

'Thirty points,' said Noel.

Henry said, 'You know, Alex really has gone magnificently.'

'You're telling me,' said Christo.

'Sorry,' said Alex, joining them.

'Oh, for heaven's sake stop apologizing,' said Henry. 'You jumped the double gates perfectly. What more do you want?'

'It's all over,' said Noel rather sadly.

'Yes, we may as well box the horses,' said Henry.

'Oh, no. Supposing you've won something,' objected Christo. 'You might have easily.'

'Sez you,' replied Henry sceptically.

'But, honestly, you've no idea how badly some people did the dressage test,' said Christo. 'It's true that I didn't see everyone and that I'm in a bit of a muddle about which teams did well in the cross-country, but still, there are going to be rosettes to fourth place and there were only six teams.'

'Oh, all right then,' said Henry; 'but we'll water them and give them the rest of the oats.' A scarlet-coated figure turned to ask if they knew that the dressage results were out; they were posted up by the secretary's tent. Thanking him, they led their tired horses along and approached the notice-board in fear and trepidation.

'My needle's come back,' observed Noel.

'You look, Cristo,' said Henry. 'Begin at the bottom.'

'Captain Leamington on Sky Blue – – minus 41 marks
S. R. Penhurst – – – – – minus 47 marks
Mrs. Hope-Gordon – – – – minus 57 marks
Miss Dingley – – – – – – minus 59 marks
Miss Kettering – – – – – – minus 60 marks,'

read Christo, ignoring Henry and beginning at the top of the list.

'Gosh! Noel's fifth,' said Alex.

'Go on,' said Henry. '

'Major Carpenter – – – – minus 63 marks
H. Thornton – – – – – – minus 69½ marks
A. Turner – – – – – – minus 72 marks.'

'Hurray,' said Henry. 'I say, Christo, they are given in order of merit, aren't they?'

'Yes, rather,' said Christo. 'Some of the people at the bottom of the list are minus 180 marks.'

'I'm stupefied with amazement,' said Alex.

Noel felt so pleased that she couldn't think of anything to say; she turned and patted Sonnet.

'You must have got something,' said Christo. 'I'm going to find out when the results will be announced.'

The final results, the secretary told Christo, would be given out about half an hour after the jumping competition had ended.

'We've ages to wait, then,' said Henry when he was told this. 'Come on, let's give these poor horses their feeds.'

When the horses were munching contentedly the Radney team, whose appetite had returned, ate all the rest of their provisions and then they wandered back to the ringside to see how the jumping was going. Someone had just fallen off; his horse had refused the second of the double gates.

'He's the last competitor,' said Christo, looking him up in the programme. Henry said that perhaps Christo was right and they had better bridle the horses. Nearly everyone else seemed to be mounting and at least they would be able to see over the heads of the spectators.

'In a moment,' announced the loudspeaker, 'we shall be able to give you the final results.'

The Radney people rushed for their horses. They were only just back in time.

'First, the Radney Riding Club with a total of 299½ minus marks,' said the loudspeaker. 'Second, Letchdale "A" team.'

'Did he say we were first?' asked Alex.

Henry's mouth was open.

'Yes, you've won,' shrieked Christo suddenly, and she slapped Noel on the back.

'Ow,' yelled Noel.

'Shush,' said Henry. 'He's still announcing.'

'—Fourth, the Downland Dressage Group with minus 334 marks.'

'The Flintshires were third,' said Alex.

'And here is the order of individual placings,' announced the microphone.

FIRST	Captain Leamington riding Sky Blue	minus 43	marks
SECOND	Mrs. Hope-Gordon riding Montrose	minus 61	marks
THIRD	S. R. Penhurst riding Colonel Marble's Truculent	minus 73	marks
FOURTH	Miss N. Kettering riding Sonnet	minus 78	marks
FIFTH	Major Carpenter riding April	minus 85	marks
SIXTH	A. Turner riding H. Thornton's Trappist	minus 92	marks.'

The announcer read solemnly through the list. Henry was

eighth with minus 129½. The Radney people were beside themselves with joy. Alex said that he just couldn't believe it and
Noel said she was dreaming, and in a minute she would wake up.
Henry said he had never been so surprised in his life, and Christo
remarked that they would never have been first with her in the
team. Then the loudspeaker began to call for the winning teams
and individuals to come into the dressage arena. With the greys
one on either side of Echo they rode in. They were told to line
up opposite the judges' platform. The Duchess of Letchdale,
carrying an enormous challenge cup and three red rosettes, bore
down upon them.

'Noel, you've got to take it, you're the only girl,' said Henry in
an urgent whisper.

'No, you take it,' said Noel. 'You're the captain of the team.
Besides, I know I shall drop it. Go on, Henry, you must.'

As the Duchess was already hovering indecisively in front of
them, Henry took it.

'Thank you very much indeed,' he said in reply to her con-
gratulations.

Alex suddenly realized that he was wearing a hat and snatched
it off as he was handed his rosette. One of the judges – he had a
foreign accent – asked them their ages and another judge asked
them who had taught them to ride. By that time the other teams
had been given their rosettes. So Henry turned and they led the
way out of the arena. Noel and Alex were soon sent in again to
receive their fourth and sixth rosettes. Sonnet's was green and
Trappist's white. Christo, who had badgered some lump sugar
out of the tea-tent staff, rewarded them as they came out of the
arena.

A horsy-looking woman was asking Henry if he wanted to sell
Echo and a very talkative and rather boring man was telling Noel
about a polo pony he had had in India which had looked just like
Sonnet, when Major Holbrooke and General de Veriac appeared.

'This is a very unexpected pleasure,' said Major Holbrooke,
solemnly shaking hands all round. 'I only saw your cross-country
and show jumping, but you put up some nice performances, and
to win the whole competition was really a remarkably good
effort.'

'Yes, I agree. And the dressage it also was very good,' said

General de Veriac. 'I think some hard work has been going on since my visit to you last month. I see great improvement and truly, from my heart, I congratulate you, for it is not easy to do these things. One thing I wish to ask,' the General continued. 'The chairman, I remember; this young lady, who today was not in such a hurry; and Mademoiselle Christo, I remember also. But this young man – I do not think I had the pleasure of instructing him?'

'No, you're quite right,' answered Henry. 'Alex is one of the younger ones, and he wasn't as good then as he is now. He used to belong to what we call the second string, but Noel's been teaching him and when Christo's horse went lame we thought he was the best person to have in the team.'

'I must, then, also congratulate Mademoiselle Noel on her teaching,' said the General.

'But this is the lunatic boy who rode the grey,' said Major Holbrooke. 'I remember him now. He gave all the cross-country judges heart-attacks. He took the drop fence at a hundred miles an hour and finished the course upside down on his horse's neck. Did you say Noel taught him? Oh, well, that accounts for his behaviour.'

The General walked with the Radney people to their horse-box talking to Henry and Christo about the excellence of that type of competition. Noel was still unable to speak, Alex was engrossed in his own thoughts and the Major, muttering something about an occasion which demanded a celebration, had disappeared. He joined them several minutes later just as they had boxed the horses, and he was carrying a half-bottle of champagne, which he poured into the challenge cup.

And, when the softening rays of the sinking sun were turning the world gold and the giant shadows of the trees were lengthening and merging across the park, the celebrators stood in a circle and each in turn they drank. They drank to the horses, to the riding club and to horsemanship. They drank to the team, and the Major, grinning at Henry, drank to Echo's success in the Olympic trials next year.

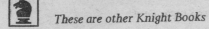

Two books about life and riding on
the Hungarian Plains, by Kate Seredy.

THE GOOD MASTER

The famous story about Uncle Marton and
his family, and his niece Kate, who comes
to live with them.

THE SINGING TREE

It is wartime, and Uncle Marton goes away
to fight, leaving his son Jancsi in charge of
the ranch.

Both books are newly illustrated by the notable
artist Imre Hofbauer who, like the author, was
born in Hungary and knows the life so
finely presented here.

William Mayne and Dick Caesar

THE GOBBLING BILLY

A little-known book by the famous writer
Entertaining and amusing and set in Ireland, this
story tells about the refurbishing of a dilapidated
vintage car, the Gobbling Billy, in time to enter
for the Bemberger Trophy race.

Bob, its owner, has to work in secrecy, and his task
is further complicated by the efforts of a rival
to ensure he doesn't win the race.

Elizabeth Goudge

LINNETS AND VALERIANS

'How to sum up the flavour of this long,
exhilarating, beautifully written book . . .?
Four children (mother dead, father in India).
Scholarly bachelor uncle decides – with aid
of wise old gardener-factotum – to educate them.
But beware of Lion Tor, and the mist when it
takes strange shapes over Weeping Marsh. And
where is Lady Valerian's lost explorer husband?
Thrilling stuff; quotable, too, all along, if
there were space.'

The Observer

'Can be enjoyed by children and adults alike.'

The Times Literary Supplement

Jane Duncan

CAMERONS ON THE HILLS

The Camerons, 13-year-old Shona, and her
brothers Neil and Donald, go to their
aunt's house in the Scottish Highlands
to stay. The place is mountainous, often
hedged in with mist, and a marvellous holiday
turns to tragedy with the crash of a plane
nearby. How the Camerons cope with this
disaster makes a ringing climax to the story.

These are other Knight Books

More books about horses and riding

Primrose Cumming
Four rode home

Monica Edwards
Rennie goes riding

Ruby Ferguson
Jill's gymkhana
A stable for Jill
Jill has two ponies
Jill and the perfect pony
Jill's riding club

Mary Treadgold
The Heron Ride

Ask your local bookseller, or at your public
library, for details of other Knight Books,
or write to the Editor-in-Chief, Knight Books,
Arlen House, Salisbury Road, Leicester, LE1 7QS.